ANGEL
on my back

DAVID A. ESTES

Cover Design: Jaycee DeLorenzo

Paperback-Press
an imprint of A & S Publishing
A & S Holmes, Inc.

ISBN-10: 1-945669-03-9
ISBN-13: 978-1-945669-03-3

CHAPTER 1

On the Banks of the Mediterranean

Long ago in a faraway land there lived an angel named Gabriel. Gabriel's career as an angel was a disaster. Gabriel squandered his chances for advancement at promotion time because of his lackadaisical perception of angelism. Passed over in favor of other, less talented, angels who tended more eagerly toward followship, Gabriel floundered in a hotbed of apathy, mystified as to why he was no longer invited to the weekly angel meetings.

Much of Gabriel's time was devoted to lounging nude on the banks of the Great Sea. That's where he was sunning himself the day his ears were attacked by the sound of a stern, authoritative voice, ear-shattering as an echo from the bowels of an empty cavern.

"Gabriel!"

Shaken with fright, Gabriel's bare skin began to crinkle. He glanced about, seeking the source of the commanding voice, but found none.

He spotted a small white cloud floating overhead, which he was pretty sure had emitted no such voice. However, he decided he had better pay attention, because whoever owned the voice sounded like he expected to be listened to.

"Yea, Lord," said Gabriel through trembling lips. With shaky hands he scurried for his robe to cover his naked body. "Here am I."

"I have need of you," said the voice.

"Need of me, Lord?" Gabriel sought a body to go with the voice, but there was none. "Who are you?"

"I am the Commander."

"The Commander?"

"Of the Universe. Are you familiar with Abraham, Isaac, and Jacob?"

"Oh, yes, sir. Didn't they play for the Yankees?"

"They were the seeds from which grew the twelve tribes of Israel. Before they were, I was."

Gabriel drew the robe closer around his shivering body.

"Who—who—did you say you were—sir?"

"I am the Commander of the Universe."

"Oh. The Commander of the Universe?"

"You better believe it."

"And you have need of me, Commander of the Universe—sir?"

"I do."

"Well–uh—why—how did you know where to find me?"

From the throat of Him Who knew all, escaped a tolerant chuckle.

"Your name popped up," said He, "as I was surfing the net."

"You, my Lord?" said the incredulous angel. "You were surfing the net?"

"In search of a man."

"And did you find him?"

"Not yet. I keep busy with other stuff 24/7. That's why I need you."

"Why me, Lord?"

"I have chosen you from the angel band as one who will do my bidding without question."

"But I am not much of an angel," Gabriel protested.

"I know."

"I haven't been able to find my halo, and my wings have rusted from lack of use."

"I know all about that, but you'll do," said He with strained patience. "Listen to me when I talk to you. Now, how would you like to be my Archangel?"

"Oh, sir! For that wouldn't you want someone with more experience, maybe even one who is perfect? I mean—I 'm not perfect."

"True." With divine modesty, He added, "Only I am perfect. But there is One to come Who is without blemish."

"Really? Who?"

"Well— But that's another story. Right now I need you to do a few errands for me."

Reflecting on that long ago first encounter, Gabriel, grown older and wiser, recalled the "errands" he was assigned. They included interpreting for a man named Daniel a dream involving a ram and a he-goat; striking dumb a temple priest named Zacharia who scoffed at the notion that his eighty-year-old wife Elizabeth would give birth to a son, John the Baptist. The assignment Gabriel most cherished was informing a young virgin named Mary that she would become the mother of Jesus, the Savior of the world.

"The world," the Commander said to the newly appointed Archangel, "is going to hell in a hand basket."

"To hell, my Lord?"

"In a hand basket."

"And what, pray tell, has that to do with me, Commander, sir?"

"I need you to contact Planet Earth, my most prized creation—though it has become dreadfully corrupt—and locate a man named Jacob Hannity."

"Jacob Hannity?"

"A despicable character. I've had my eye on him for some time, but he doesn't answer when I call. Once a good man, he now is totally worthless, thinking only of himself. Rescued from his wasteful endeavors, he will be perceived as a prime example of what a scoundrel can become with proper training, accomplishing good for people who can't do for themselves, spreading love and joy, shining the light of peace and happiness where dankness now prevails."

"Oh, sir! Wouldn't you—"

"Find Hannity, Gabriel, and report back to me."

"But, my Lord, how am I to find a man I don't know, on a planet that's going to hell—"

"In a hand basket."

"—in a hand basket, a man who is totally worthless, who thinks only of himself?"

"Good question, Gabe. There are so many of them down there. Sleazy politicians, crooked salesmen, scam artists. Selfish, arrogant, egotistical. Hannity likely will not be one of high office, but you will recognize him when you find him."

"But, my Lord—"

"You're not gonna crawfish on me here, are you, Gabe?"

"Oh, no, sir—but—"

"Remember Saul of Tarsus?"

"Yes, sir, I remember him all right." Gabriel wondered what he and Saul had in common.

"A scoundrel from the git-go, Saul was," said the Commander. "Still, after he was struck blind, and became the Apostle Paul, he was my greatest messenger.

"Hannity is no Apostle Paul," He conceded ruefully, "but with proper guidance he could be transformed into somebody useful."

The Commander paused for a thoughtful moment, then said, "The world I created is in turmoil, Gabe, with no shame, no remorse, no regret. That upstart Greek, Epicurus, poisoned the minds of my people with his philosophy of materialism and narcissism, and now the country I love, and to which I give most, has turned against me. The people have fallen into disrespect, not for me only, but for each other, engaging in slander, scandal, and corruption."

"Dare I ask, sir, to which country you refer?"

"You may dare. It is bound on the east and west

by mighty bodies of water, and on the north and south by nations whose friendship is tenuous at best."

"Then, sir—"

"You are not too young to remember the Flood?"

"Oh, no, sir, I remember the Flood. That's when you destroyed the world, saving only Noah and his family aboard the ark with all those dirty animals stinking up the place, and—"

"An evil world, Gabe. A world that had forsaken me. I had no choice but to destroy it and start all over."

Gabriel gave his head a reflective nod.

"How many angels have we?" said the Commander.

"I—I don't know, sir. Thousands? Maybe a million?"

"I know how many there are. I considered sending them all down there to wipe from the face of the earth the country I love whose people, even so, rise up against me, marching in protest of all things good, desecrating my Commandments, denying children the right to be children."

"My Lord!"

"Evil must be obliterated, Gabe, so once again there will be time and space for good in the world."

"But, if it is the country you love, is there not some means short of destruction to cleanse it of evil?"

"Not until the Savior returns, and I alone know when that will be."

"The savior, sir?"

"My boy, Jesus. Only I know when he will come again."

"Well, when?"

"The world is not yet ready for him, Gabe. I refuse to subject my Son to a world of conflict, oppression, wars and rumors of wars, to be spat upon, mocked, and crucified over and over again!

"Search the land, Gabriel, and find for me the man whom I can rescue from an ungrateful world, and transform into an example of people who care about each other, who are tolerant and considerate of the poor and downtrodden, who love each other as I love them."

"May I ask, sir—"

"Find Jacob Hannity for me, Gabe," the voice shouted, fading into the distance, "then await further instructions!"

Gabriel watched the white cloud melt into the atmosphere. For a frightening moment he meditated, muttering to himself, "And where in the name of the Commander of the Universe shall I begin to look for a man in a wide, wicked world I've never seen—a man named Hannity who probably doesn't want to be found?"

Despite the Commander's obvious distaste for "men of high office," the Archangel set out on his mission to ascertain the whereabouts of Jacob Hannity, a scoundrel fingered by the Commander for transformation into an instrument for good, capable of improving the dreadful plight of humanity in the country He most loved.

Abiding by the instructions of the Commander,

Gabriel's diligent search discovered among plumbers, ditch diggers, barbers, brick layers, bakers, and myriad other workers none who answered to the name of Jacob Hannity. There were Joseph Hannity, Caleb Hannity, Kevin, Angus, even one male Hannity who claimed to be Lucille, but not one who admitted to being Jacob Hannity.

Not even in the ranks of the ACLU did he uncover the lowest of the lowly. He expanded his search to include men of the cloth, bankers, lawyers, executives of major corporations, and congressmen and senators from thirty-seven states.

At the end of his frustrating rope, Gabriel was forced to admit to the Commander that he failed in his efforts to ferret out the elusive Jacob Hannity.

"He's there, Gabe!" the Commander roared. "Find him!"

Finally, lowering his sights to bedrock, Gabriel was astonished to discover the man at whom the Commander of the Universe had pointed the Finger of Destiny—swallowing an ice pick.

CHAPTER 2

The Ice Pick Swallower

Three months ago Jacob Hannity lost his wife Nancy to leukemia. He thought himself a pretty tough guy whom nothing could bring down. He found out losing Nancy was a load he wasn't tough enough to handle. Added to that, a month after she died, he was "furloughed" from his job at the Nuts & Bolts Warehouse. His world became a vacuum he no longer cared to fight his way out of.

Hannity never claimed to be a state-of-the-art husband, but he truly loved Nancy. He watched her suffer through months of emaciating pain, and knew there had to be a better way to go. He went looking for it.

Alone in a world that held for him little promise, Jake waged war against the loneliness that stalked him like a hungry hound wherever he went.

As an alternative he turned to his friend Jack Daniel's, seeking refuge on the bottom of the barrel of humanity. Searching for something to fill the void left by the loss of his beloved wife, he began a campaign to obliterate all sense of feeling.

Reality was something other people talked about. Jacob did his best to out run it. It was a sad day when he sold the house he and Nancy moved into the year they were married.

He loaded up the old Chevy camper he and Frank Stickney, John Salash, and Tom Bugler used to fill with beer and burgers for weekends of fishing and hunting. With his brown beagle Bogey on the seat beside him, he took off for parts unknown. Literally.

He pointed the camper's nose north with no idea where sundown would find him. His only thought was getting away from people and places that reminded him of his sorrow, expecting nothing good to happen along the way.

Night times Jake parked his camper at highway rest areas, clearings in the woods, or at KOA's.

One night he found himself in a neighborhood bar in Delavan, Wisconsin. Some prankster on the stool next to him dared Jake to swallow an ice pick. Jake had downed enough alcohol to drown a big-mouth bass, so he tried.

Egged on by thrill-seeking bystanders as soused as he, Jake threw his head back and poised the sharp end of the ice pick above his mouth.

That was when he heard the voice.

"Jacob."

It was no ordinary voice, sounding like it came from far away, like an echo he and Nancy marveled at bouncing off the walls of the Grand Canyon. Jake heard it as plainly as if it came from the man on the next stool. He looked around, expecting to see who called his name, but he knew nobody among the revelers, nor did they know who he was.

Jake shook it off, thinking he must be "hearing things." Once again he poised the ice pick above his mouth.

"Jacob."

There it was again. For reasons he couldn't explain, Jake looked up, scanning the whitewashed ceiling, as though expecting to find a face that matched the voice. All he saw were fogs of cigarette smoke filling the room.

"If you're foolish enough to try swallowing an ice pick," the authoritative voice said, "at least have the good sense to insert the butt end first."

Jake was recognized among friends as a toper who could consume enough alcohol to float a johnboat and still walk away without falling on his face. There were times, though, in his loop-legged oblivion, when he dredged up weird images of snakes and tarantulas, and even skinless, cackling Harpies wielding torches and pitchforks. He thought this must be one of those times.

The ice pick began to quiver in his hand. Even loaded to the gills, Jake was lucid enough to wonder whether his mind might be slipping away. He had heard tales of people with taunting little voices shattering the walls of their minds. But this was no little voice. This one was deep and calm and patient, like no voice he had ever heard.

"Jacob."

Suddenly the ice pick went flying, and Jake was yanked off the barstool by some invisible force.

Arms flailing away, he was lifted by the scruff of the neck and the seat of his pants, and sent sailing out the door.

The jeering spectators thought Jake was in the throes of a drunken seizure. A gale of derisive laughter followed him onto the street, and to his camper parked down the block.

He crawled into the cab of his truck and slumped over the wheel, exhausted as if he had just crossed the finish line of a 10K marathon. He fumbled in his pocket for his keys, but they weren't there. He couldn't remember what he was supposed to do next. What was happening to him?

"Jacob."

"What!"

"You need not yell. I can hear you."

"Who are you?"

"Are you all right?"

"What are you trying to do to me?"

"I had to get you out of that place. Those people were making an ass of you."

"Why are you picking on me?"

"I am not picking on you," said the faceless, bodiless voice. "If you had seen how ridiculous you looked trying to swallow that ice pick, you would never take another drink for as long as you live."

"That's none of your business!"

"You are my business."

"No, I am not your business, whoever you are. What are you—some kind of ventriloquist? I don't need any funny little games right now. Just get off my back and leave me alone."

"Very well. Perhaps we can talk another time

when you're in a more positive frame of mind."

Jake felt something drop onto his lap. "What's that?" he said.

"Your keys. You left them on the bar."

Jake couldn't believe it. "My keys?" He thought he really was losing his mind. "Who did you say you were?"

"I didn't say. However, who I am is of no consequence at this point. What's more important is who you are."

"What the hell!"

"Please, do not utter that word in my presence. Where I come from we have no regard for such a place."

"Well, I don't know where you come from, but since you seem to know everything else, you must know who I am."

"True. I also know you are a disgusting human being."

"Now, wait a minute!"

"I know you were once a good man who now has no regard for anyone but himself. I know you are a slobbering, disgusting drunk, Jacob Hannity. I also know you frequently frittered away the family savings, and brought pain to your loving wife Nancy."

"Nancy?" he gulped, his voice a whisper. "You know about Nancy?"

"I know about Nancy. I know you were married to her seventeen years. I know she wanted children, but you complained that children would hamper your lifestyle. You were too busy indulging in what pleased you, instead of her."

"I loved Nancy," Jake said, trying to mount a defense. "I wasn't the world's greatest maybe, but I was a good husband."

"Oh?"

"I used to bring her Stover's candy because she loved chocolate. And I always gave her something for her birthday. Surely you remember that."

"Don't be smart, Jacob. I remember the watch you gave her on her last birthday. You got it on sale at Walmart for less than the price of a good bass lure. You gave her things, Jacob, but you rarely gave of yourself, which was all she ever wanted. Much of the time you were off carousing with your buddies. Even in her final days when she needed you most, where were you?"

"Well, I was—"

"Never mind. I know where you were. And that lady named Lonni knows too."

"Lonni?" Jake said, aghast. "You—you know about Lonni?"

"And Millicent, and Loretta, and Julia, and— Shall I go on?"

"That didn't mean anything to me."

"It meant plenty to Nancy."

"She never knew."

"Believe me, Jacob, she knew."

Incredulous, Jacob said, "Who—who are you?"

"I am Gabriel, the Archangel."

"The what? The ark—"

"—angel."

"I don't believe you."

"Whether or not you believe me renders it no less true. I've been instructed to recruit you for a special mission down there."

"Down here?"

"From where I am, everything is down.

"The record shows you've lived forty-two years, and you have very little to show for it. I see greed, self-indulgence, wasted time and talent, and a complete lack of consideration for your fellow man, except when it brings you something in return."

"Now, hold on there!"

"Because of your irresponsible worthlessness, you are perfect for the job I have in mind for you."

"I have a job."

"You had a job, but you lost it because you often didn't show up for work, and when you did put in an appearance, you often got someone else to do it for you."

"It wasn't my fault."

"Please, Jacob, don't whine."

"But, you should have been there when I grew up."

"I was."

"Then you must know — you were?"

"Before time was, I was."

"My father abused me, and my mother locked me in the closet until I stopped crying. Then, if I didn't stop—"

"You're whining, Jacob."

"You just don't get it, do you?"

"You weren't listening, Jacob. Do you realize with whom you're speaking?"

"Okay, so you're Gabriel Whoever, and you know everything, so you must know it wasn't easy growing up the way I did."

"How old are you, Jacob?"

"You know how old I am! I'm forty-two."

"Where were you at this time last week?"

"Uh—last week? I don't remember."

"So, you can't remember where you were last week, but you can't forget what happened to you forty years ago. Don't you find that a bit disturbing?"

"It's hard."

"Of course, it's hard, but you're a big boy now. You need to get over it, accept responsibility for what you do with your life. Stop looking back, remembering the bad things, and start looking ahead to the good stuff."

"The good stuff?"

"Isn't that what you call it?"

"Yeah, the good stuff."

"Now, are we ready to talk business?"

"I—I— don't know. What kind of job is it?"

"From time-to-time," the angel said, "I will contact you with an assignment you must perform without question. You will be advised where to go, whom to see, and what to do once you arrive there."

"You say you're an angel—with wings?"

"The angel part is correct. The wings are not a matter of concern."

"I don't know about this."

"What don't you know about, Jacob?"

"Would I have to wear a long white robe?"

"Of course not. You can even dress as sloppily as you are now if you prefer—army surplus dungarees and dirty sneakers. The Commander doesn't care what you look like."

"The commander?"

"He's my boss. And yours if things work out."

"No wings, no halo either?"

"Cute, Jacob."

While Jacob mulled it over, Gabriel began questioning whether he could handle this or any other assignment he may be called upon to perform. "Maybe you're not right for this job, after all," Gabriel said. "And I'll have to take back the money you won with that lottery ticket."

How could he know about the lottery ticket? Foolish question. "You know about that?" said Jake, no longer surprised.

"You couldn't have done it without me."

"You fixed the lottery?"

"Let's say I arranged it. Or fixed it, if you prefer. I gave you the idea of stopping at that Seven-Eleven where you bought the winning ticket. The money you won you will share with people less fortunate than yourself."

For Jake that was a head scratcher. Who could be less fortunate than he?

"I will not burden you with an explanation of where the money now resides," said the Archangel, "but, of course, I will be in charge of how it is dispensed. Each case will be dealt with individually as the need is determined."

"Wait a minute! That's my money."

"No, Jacob, it is not your money. You are only the instrument by whom the Commander's mission is meant to accomplish."

"I paid good money for that ticket!"

"And you shall be reimbursed fully for the

purchase price."

"I think you'd better be getting somebody else to do your dirty work."

"If I do that, you will have missed a rare opportunity to rise above the nothingness you now are."

"I don't think I can live with your supercilious attitude."

"Get used to it, Jacob. It could get worse."

"You haven't explained why you put the finger on me for what's going on here."

"I told you. You're a worthless human being."

"Then why did you choose me for the job?"

"I did not choose you. I only found you. Left to me, you'd have been at the bottom of the list, but when the Commander makes up His mind, experience has taught me that debate is futile.

"You're a bum, Jacob. Look at that frowzy head of long hair that hasn't been trimmed in weeks. That beer breath of yours would stifle a dinosaur. And your army surplus dungarees wouldn't pass inspection at a Rolling Stones cook-out.

"Even so, in you the Commander recognizes potential for good you have not allowed to escape your self-centered shell. You must be somebody, as they say, 'cause God don't make no trash.

"You were chosen by the Commander Himself, not for what you are, but for what you might become."

"Well," Jake said meekly, "maybe I have done some pretty dumb things."

"That's interesting. There may be hope for you

yet. Once you admit to having made mistakes, you're on the road to recovery."

Jake's mind was in a swirl of confusion. There seemed no escape from this taunting voice, except to yield to it. He was not pleased with his resignation, but escape loomed like a shroud of futility. "All right, I—" he said. 'What do you want me to do?"

"Now we're getting somewhere. Stay alert, and I'll get back to you. Goodbye for now."

"Wait!" Gabriel scared the devil out of him, but Jake wasn't ready for him to disappear. "What am I supposed to do?"

"In due time, Jacob," said Gabriel as his voice trailed off. "In due time."

CHAPTER 3

The Bank Deposit

Jake looked across the paneled enclosure at a nattily dressed, bespectacled man of fifty-four. He didn't like his haughty, self-righteous appearance, but figured Gabriel knew what he was doing when he gave him this assignment.

The name plate on the edge of the desk told him the man's name was "Mr. Foster," but he asked anyway. "Are you Mr. Foster?"

"Yes, sir. How may I help you?"

"They told me over there you could help me open a checking account."

"Indeed I can, sir. We're always pleased to welcome a new depositor. Won't you have a seat?"

Jake stood. "I just want to put some money in an account for—" He consulted a scrap of paper with a name scribbled on it. "Mary Ann Bracker."

Mr. Foster swiveled around to his computer and typed something into it. "And how much would you like to deposit in the name of Mary Ann

Bracker?"

"I thought ten thousand would be enough for a start," Jake answered.

Mr. Foster peered over the tops of his black horn-rimmed spectacles, greeting Jake's words with a dubious nod. "Ten thousand." He swiveled back to his computer, trying to convince himself that this bedraggled individual staring down at him from the other side of his desk had ever seen ten thousand dollars.

"Is that Miss or Mrs. Bracker?" Foster asked.

"I'm sure it's Mrs. I know she has kids."

From a pocket of his dungarees, Jake brought a wad of money and started peeling off hundred-dollar bills.

Foster's eyes grew big at sight of the greenbacks piling up on his desk. "What is—Mrs.—Bracker's address?" he asked.

"I'm not real sure," Jake said, "but there was something about Mobile Village."

Mr. Foster knew about Mobile Village. Though his feet had never trod what he had been told was its contaminated soil, his perception of Mobile Village was a collection of nondescript mobile homes scattered about on the west side of town. He "had heard" also that the police were frequently called there by women who bore scars of abuse by drunken husbands or jealous boyfriends. For a sophisticated banker, Mobile Village was a place to be avoided like smallpox.

"Are you familiar with Mobile Village?" the banker asked with a superior tone of voice.

"No, I'm from out of town, but I thought you

might find out where she lives and notify her of the bank account."

"Mrs.—Bracker," said Mr. Foster with a quizzical appraisal of the dungareed Jake. "Is she a friend of yours, a member of your family? What exactly is—"

Foster's arrogant, holier than thou attitude shot Jake's patience meter to near the red flag flipping zone. "What exactly is the problem here?" he said. "Is there some reason why I can't put money in your bank for anybody I want?"

"Well, it's highly unusual you would open an account for someone whose name you know, but whose address you do not know, and who is neither a relative nor a friend."

"Are you saying you don't want my money because I don't know the person I'm depositing it for?"

"What I'm saying is you are not a customer of the bank, sir. We don't know who you are, nor where the money came from."

"Well, let me tell you something, sir. Until a couple of minutes ago I didn't know who you were either, but I never challenged your integrity. And as to whether you're a man of honor, I gave you the benefit of the doubt. My name is Jacob Hannity. You may not like the way I look, but this is clean money."

He began scooping the bills off Mr. Foster's desk. "I came by it honestly, and there's a lot more where this came from, and I can assure you, sir, that neither you nor your bank will ever see any of it again." Jake stuffed the bills back in his pocket, and showed the stunned, wide-eyed banker his back as he left.

On his way out, Jake felt the furtive glances of critical-eyed employees hovering over their desks, observing his departure without moving their heads. He suspected they were thinking there should be a law prohibiting such rubbish from entering their pristine bank.

Jake was not impressed. He wondered if Gabriel was up there some place smiling his approval of how well he handled that situation with Mr. Foster.

Since Mr. Foster reacted as if his money were fraught with germs of some communicable disease —and was no more complimentary of Mobile Village—Jake decided to deliver the money to Mary Ann Bracker himself.

He hailed a man on a street corner and asked directions to Mobile Village. The man told him how to get there, had nothing good to say about the village, and hurried away as though avoiding contact with a leper.

Jake didn't know Mary Ann Bracker from Cleopatra, but the more trash he heard about Mobile Village, and Mary Ann by association, the more determined he became to find it and her. Actually, he had little choice but to go in search of Mary Ann, since that was the first assignment Gabriel laid upon him, and it was too late to back out.

He was driving to Mobile Village minding his own business with Bogey panting with his pink tongue hanging out on the seat beside him. Out of the blue came the voice of the Archangel, chastising him for his unacceptable behavior in his encounter with Mr. Foster at the bank.

"You didn't handle that very well, Jacob," said the angel. "You were supposed to deposit the money in the bank."

"Well, I never did get along well with stuffed shirts."

"That's not surprising," said the Archangel. "Tolerance is a scarce commodity among new recruits. However, you are allowed only one more indiscretion. If you exceed that, it may necessitate my reporting your behavior to the Commander."

"Report me? Don't break my heart." Jake thought he sounded defiant, which probably was not the proper approach with the Archangel, but it adequately expressed his feelings. "I didn't ask for this job, you know"

"True. But the fact that you are here is proof of your acceptance. And once you've earned your way into the Fold, there are certain guidelines by which your behavior will be monitored."

"The fold?"

"Yes. If you prove worthy, you will become a member of the Commander's Flock."

"What flock? You mean like sheep?"

"Do you have a problem with that?"

"Well," Jake said, as if resigning himself to the inevitable. "I've come this far."

"Good. I assume you still have the money."

"You're talking about the ten thousand?"

"Yes."

"That's a lot of money to lay on a woman I don't know."

"Your job is not to know her, but to lay it on her, as you say. Just try to remember it's not your money, and it won't be so difficult."

"I don't know."

"Don't worry about it, Jacob. If you need help, just call."

"Yeah, well, I've called a couple of times already and you didn't answer."

"Jacob."

"I'm not cut out for this kind of work."

"Just remember, if you complete this assignment in a satisfactory manner, you improve your chances of being accepted into the Fold."

"Well, that fold is something else that doesn't sound right to me. I mean—how do I know you're who you say you are? Have you got any ID? Social Security number, driver's license? You go around telling people you're the Archangel, but you never show your face. And the kind of stuff you're asking me to do—"

"Needless to say, I agree you are not suited for this assignment. Even so, in you the Commander sees something worth saving, and when He speaks, He leaves no room for debate. What I think is not important, but what you think is, and as long as you perceive yourself as a worthless bum, a worthless bum is all you will ever be. My task is to transform you from a despicable wine bibber into a respectable human being worthy of the Commander's regard.

"Now, pull yourself together, Jacob. There's work to be done—to be done—to be—"

"Gabriel!"

CHAPTER 4

Jake Visits Mobile Village

Mary Ann Bracker was the mother of three young children.

She caught the attention of the Commander, Gabriel explained to Jacob, because she lost her husband in an accident at the paper mill. Mary Ann lost her job at the shoe factory, falling victim to what the manager labeled "downsizing." Even so, Mary Ann continued to share what little she had, caring for the sick and elderly in her neighborhood who were even less fortunate than she.

Jake knew what "downsizing" meant. It happened to him. Sales at the nuts and bolts warehouse took a seasonal dive, and the company solved the problem by what they called "furloughing" certain employees. Jake was one of them. He had worked at the warehouse for eighteen years. He discovered that "furloughing" was management's way of saying, "You're outta here!"

Jake admitted he hadn't been a model

employee, but losing his job was devastating, even more so because of Nancy's death.

Month after agonizing month he watched her suffer from the insidious monster that was eating her alive. He struggled with his helplessness, angry that there was nothing he could do for her. Inconsiderate and negligent as he sometimes was toward Nancy, Jake couldn't recall a day when he wasn't glad she was the woman he married.

He watched her supple body deteriorate, and agonized through her weakened spirit. He wished he could destroy all the white and blue smocks parading the halls of the hospital with masks hiding their faces, and stethoscopes bouncing off their chests.

He watched them stick their heads in the door of her hospital room, ask the insipid, "How are we doing today?" They made notes on their clipboards, and disappear with little regard for how she was really doing.

Nancy never saw the ocean. She once quipped that she would like to take a trip out west and "loll around in it like the rich folks do."

Jake wasn't good at showing affection, but neither did he ever do anything to intentionally hurt Nancy. He did some things he was sorry for, carousing with the hunting and fishing buddies he grew up with, sometimes leaving her alone on weekends.

Waylon and Willie could dedicate that song to him— the good-hearted woman in love with a good-timing man. Even so, when Jake promised Nancy someday they would load up the camper and head west to see the ocean, she knew he meant it.

They even made plans for trooping off down to the Gulf, or maybe out to California, to get a whiff of the Pacific's salt air. But, Jake lost her, and a short time later, he lost his job. That was the day he began to die.

One of his wandering days ended in Delavan, Wisconsin. For some reason he couldn't explain, he plunked down a dollar bill for a lottery ticket. In his recently adopted nomadic existence, he subscribed to the theory that the best way to deal with temptation was to let it win.

Never before had he bought a lottery ticket, one of the few moral weaknesses to which he had not succumbed. He didn't know why he bought this one at the Seven-Eleven, except that something drew him to risk the greenback.

Flashed across the screen of the television behind the bar where he came to keep an appointment with Jack Daniel's, Jake saw the winning lottery numbers. He casually dragged out of a shirt pocket the ticket he paid a dollar for and compared it to the numbers on the screen.

He couldn't totally comprehend what his bleary eyes were trying to make him believe. The hand that held the ticket began to shake. His eyes got as big as golf balls. He slid off the barstool, made a dash for the camper, and headed down the road to the Seven-Eleven where he bought the ticket.

The gray-haired man behind the counter took his ticket and ran it through the scanner. His face lit up even brighter than Jake's. "Hot damn!" he yelled. "We got ourselves a winner here!"

Jake Hannity just won $3,000,000 from his one dollar investment. His heart pounded so he thought it might beat a hole in his dungarees.

The gray-haired man explained to Jake how to collect his winnings. Jake cut a bee-line back to the bar. He was bursting to tell someone his good news, but there was no one he cared to share it with. His head was in a whirl with a list of all the things he could do with his new-found fortune. He wished Nancy were there to help him spend it. It was at that point his drunken neighbor on the stool next to him dared Jake to swallow the ice pick.

The narrow gravel street of Mobile Village wound around a smattering of single-wide and double-wide mobile homes anchored thirty feet apart. Between them were strewn discarded charcoal grills, lawn chairs with no backs, bicycles with no wheels. Styrofoam coolers, old refrigerators, gas stoves, and microwaves, cast off like dirty underwear, scattered about as if dropped from a hot air balloon. Parked with no plan of uniformity were canvas-covered fishing boats, pickups and campers of various makes and models, mostly Fords and Chevys, with trailer hitches attached to rear bumpers. Mounted on every roof was a TV antenna.

Jake had no idea which of the mobile homes belonged to Mary Ann Bracker. Slowly he steered the camper along the gravel street, looking from side to side for someone to ask about Mary Ann.

Heads began popping out of doorways and open windows. Questioning eyes followed the approach of a stranger in a dirty camper, curiosity aroused by the clatter of pots and pans dangling from its sides.

At least, Jake said to himself, the noise stirred the inquisitive nature of at least one person. He pulled up beside a red-haired, buck-toothed young woman plopped down on her front stoop with her bare legs crossed, puffing on a cigarette.

"At the end of the street," she said to Jake's inquiry with a bright smile. "The last house on the right."

Jake thanked her, and eased on down the street until he spotted a mailbox with "Brackers" painted in red letters mounted on a post. He took a deep breath.

This was his first assignment, and, left to him, it would be his last. It didn't top the list of things he'd rather be doing. Even so, he didn't want to arouse the wrath of the Archangel. Gabriel already threatened him with a report to that commander guy if he slipped up again.

That sounded like the angel had plans for his future, but that didn't shake Jake. He had other fish to fry, and considered this caper a one-time favor to the Archangel. Once it was done, he would be on his way to parts unknown. He had a mental picture of how ridiculous Gabriel would look doing this job himself, flitting around above Mobile Village, searching for the home of Mary Ann Bracker.

Jake gave some thought to how best to handle the matter of giving her the money. He could find a bank—not Mr. Foster's—and open an account for her. Or he could place the envelope full of hundred-dollar bills in her mailbox. He tossed that idea aside, reasoning that if someone else got to the mailbox ahead of Mary Ann, she might never see the money.

What if he just walked up there and knocked on her front door and said, "Hi, I'm Jake Hannity. I'm supposed to give you ten thousand dollars," then dropped the envelope in her hands and left?

That plan got the nod.

He went to the door then gave it a good rap with his fist. A moment later he was greeted by a neatly dressed, dark-haired woman of thirty-three who appeared puzzled to be looking into the unshaven face of a man she didn't know. "Mrs. Bracker?"

"Yes?"

"I'm Jake Hannity. Someone very important knows about your recent misfortune and asked me to give you this." Whereupon he pushed the envelope into her hands, and made swift tracks back to his camper.

"Thank you," she called to his back, and began unsealing the envelope.

Jake was relieved to be rid of it. Escaping the scene, he never saw the shocked but grateful look on the face of Mary Ann Bracker.

CHAPTER 5

A Little Brown Bottle

On the night stand beside the bed stood the half empty glass from which he gulped water that washed the little white pills down his throat.

The squat, innocent-looking, half empty brown bottle lay toppled as though struck by a careless hand. A folded sheet of blue-lined white paper was leaning against the glass. Across the paper was scrawled a single word: Whoever. The message inside said only, "I'm sorry it happened this way. I never meant to hurt anyone."

Marcus Whitt would have been forty-seven years old on Thursday.

CHAPTER 6

Georgia's Dilemma

Through her kitchen window Georgia Millwood watched with disdain as the rain splattered off the sheet of blue plastic covering the pool in her back yard. For weeks, the temperature hovered around a hundred degrees, devastating her flower beds and husband James's vegetable garden.

James confessed to being "about ready to give up "on his sun-parched lawn.

Since a week ago Friday, they were victimized by what Georgia thought it must be like to live through a tropical monsoon. The first three days the rain gauge on the patio measured over seven inches, adding a burden of gloom to her worry about what was going to happen to James since his heart attack.

She hadn't checked the rain gauge since. She didn't want to know how much it rained.

The kids loved it. All four of them squealed and romped around in the rain, laughing and giggling, splashing each other until their mother called them in to "come in this house and get out of those wet clothes."

For twenty-three years her husband James worked as a lineman for the phone company. Never once did he call in sick. He boasted good-naturedly to his friends: He had never been sick a day in his life. she couldn't remember the last time he even took an aspirin.

Two weeks ago Saturday, James was digging a hole to plant a lilac bush in the yard south of the house. He collapsed with what the hospital people said was a massive heart attack.

This morning, as every morning since, on her visit to the hospital, Georgia quizzed the doctors about the seriousness of James's condition. And again they told her what she didn't want to hear. His only hope for survival was a heart transplant.

"We're searching for a donor," Dr. Finney said.

A donor! And how many thousands of dollars would that cost?

Georgia was a thirty-nine-year-old black, stay-at-home-and-take-care-of-the-kids mother. She was eighteen when she and James married, and hadn't worked a day outside the home since. With no productive skills, and James in the hospital, money was running out for feeding her kids. Most of their savings were already eaten up for hospital and doctor bills, MRI's, Cat Scans, and the Lord only knew what else.

A heart transplant?

She read everything she could find at the library, hospital, doctors' offices, and the Internet about heart attacks, including transplants. Through research and inquiry she learned the cost of a heart transplant was many thousands of dollars. She didn't have and didn't know where to look for it.

James had a good job at the phone company. Like other young couples, he and Georgia couldn't imagine the good times wouldn't last forever, nor that somewhere along the way an emergency they hadn't prepared for might rear its ugly head.

"Oh, yeah," James had assured her, "our insurance will cover that."

Then came the heart attack, and their world began to crumble. When they most needed the health coverage they thought they had—for which for years money had been deducted from James's salary—the insurance company informed them "the money well" ran dry.

What was she to do?

Georgia told her sister Belle, "I'll sell my body on the street if I have to before I'll let my kids go hungry. I can't let him die thinking I didn't do anything to help him stay alive."

The body-selling threat was made in a moment of desperation, an expression of her determination to do whatever was necessary to care for her four children.

Frustrated in attempts to find work that paid enough to support her family, and maybe make a dent in the cost of a heart transplant, Georgia concluded that becoming a greeter at Walmart was not the answer. She needed a lot of money fast. At the end of her thinking, trying and planning—and that legendary rope that frustrated people got to the end of—the street corner won. That was where Jake

Hannity found her.

All she knew about "selling my body" Georgia learned by observing other women on the street doing the same thing, women who had engaged in the endeavor of "turning tricks." Most of them were white, between twenty and forty years old, down on their luck, recovering from a divorce, drugs, or a "busted relationship," working the street because they had no earning skills and "that's where the money is."

In a tight-fitting, thigh-high black skirt and a blue top, it was her first night out. Georgia flashed a mechanical smile and stepped to the curb when the camper slowed to a stop at the curb.

Through the rolled-down passenger side window, Jake said, "How much would it take?"

"You gotta ask?" Georgia said. "For what?"

"To get you off the street."

"Is that a proposition?"

"Sort of."

She leaned toward the camper, peered in, and turned up her nose at the unshaven, long-haired, middle-aged stranger looking back at her.

"You can't afford it, man," she said.

"How much?"

"Hah!" she scoffed. "How about fifty thousand big ones?"

"Fifty thousand." Jake whistled through his teeth. "That's a lot of big ones."

"Jacob."

"I hear you," Jake whispered without moving his lips. He'd worked on that response for such occasions as this.

"Her husband is in City General awaiting a heart transplant," Gabriel said.

"You already told me that."

"I know, but she needs to know you're here to help."

To Georgia, Jake said, "I heard your call."

"My what? I didn't call anybody."

"Are you Georgia Millwood?"

"Am I who? How did you— I don't go 'round giving out my name to everybody that crawls out of the woodwork." She leaned against a lamppost. "Are you a cop?"

"No cop. We need to talk."

"Talk won't pay the bills, man."

"I might be able to help."

"Sure you can." She'd had about enough of this creep in the camper with pots and pans bouncing against its sides. "You're weird, man. Go 'way and quit bugging me."

"I have some money."

The sound of the word caused her ears to perk up. She glanced around to see if anyone was watching. From the other women she learned "the rules," including how to spot a cop with her eyes closed. Satisfied that no one was within earshot, she moved toward the camper and leaned into the curbside window.

"Jacob! Do not let that lady get in your car!" Gabriel warned.

Jake waved him off.

"Man," Georgia said with a dubious shake of her head, "you don't look like you could buy a rasslin' jacket for a flea."

Flashing lights swept Jake's rear view mirror.

"Uh-oh," Georgia said, but it was too late. How could she have missed that one?

A black-and-white police car pulled over and parked in front of the camper. Georgia wished she could melt away and disappear, but there was no time. A young black officer was already out of the car, strolling toward Jake's camper.

The officer glanced at Georgia, then said to Jake, "Good evening, sir."

"Good evening, officer," Jake said.

"I'm Officer Goodman, and I'd like to see your driver's license, please."

Jake came out with his wallet and showed it to him.

"Would you remove it from your wallet, please?"

Jake did as he was told.

Goodman glanced at the driver's license, excused himself with a nod, then turned away to his car.

Jake saw Goodman talking on the car radio. Surely he wasn't calling for backup. He hadn't done anything that called for that.

When Goodman returned, he said, "Mr. Hannity, are you aware that you could be breaking the law just by talking to this lady?"

"I don't—"

"He wasn't hitting on me, officer," Georgia said.

Goodman's instincts told him when he was being lied to, especially by the street women. Oddly, he had learned that, in spite of their plight, most of them were honest. He handed Jake's driver's license to him. "Is that true, sir?" he said.

"Yes."

Georgia said, "He said something about helping me get off the street."

Goodman moved his gaze from one face to the other. He hadn't seen this new woman before, and wondered why she was there. She was different from the others: smooth skin, bright smile, not streetwise. Like she came from a better part of town. Maybe her problems were more pressing than the others', Goodman thought. Still, if he caught her soliciting, he wouldn't hesitate to run her in.

Goodman had no clue as to how Jake planned to save her, questioning whether this shabby bum in the rattletrap camper was capable of saving anyone. But, Headquarters had nothing on him, and Jake had broken no law. "You're not from here?" he said to Jake.

"No. I'm just passing through."

"If I were you, sir, I'd keep moving. It's not safe in this part of town after dark." To Georgia, Goodman said, "You know the rules. You need to be careful too." With that, Officer Goodman climbed into his squad car and drove away.

"You're weird, man," Georgia said to Jake.

Jake shifted the camper into gear and moved out.

Georgia went back to worrying about how she was going to raise the money for James's heart transplant.

CHAPTER 7

The Angel Rescues the Sinner

Jake considered himself lucky he didn't land in jail for hobnobbing with a prostitute. He needed what he called a stiff one to settle his nerves. He swung in and parked at the first flashing neon sign he saw advertising "Bar and Grill."

He slid onto a stool, ordered Jack Daniel's on ice, wrapped a hand around the glass, and heard the snap. He felt the crunch of glass crumbling in his hand.

The bald bartender, Nathan Cloyd, shouted, "Hey, man, be careful with those glasses. They don't come cheap, you know." He noticed the blood spurting from Jake's hand. "Are you okay, man?" Nathan asked.

Jake didn't answer. He headed for the men's room with a napkin wrapped around his bleeding hand. "Okay, what have I done now?" he said to empty space.

"I'm disappointed to find you here, Jacob," said

the ubiquitous Archangel. "I thought we had an agreement you would give up drinking."

"You had an agreement, I didn't." Jake stuck his hand under the lavatory spout and heard the red stream gurgle down the drain. He ripped a handful of brown paper towel from the dispenser. "What do you want from me?" he said.

"I'm trying to save you because the Commander believes you are worth the trouble."

"Commander shammander! Who does he think he is?"

"He knows who he is. The question is, do you know who you are?"

"I'm a drunken bum! You said so yourself."

"Jacob."

"A gutter rat." He ran his cupped hands full of water and splashed it on his face. "The scum of the earth!" He mopped his face with the paper towels.

"Jacob, listen to me!"

Jake didn't like the impatience he heard in the voice of the Archangel. He let Gabriel know he was not the only upset participant in the conversation. "Okay," he said, "I'm listening."

"I've got something at stake here too," the angel said. "If I fail to execute this mission to the Commander's satisfaction, I could be demoted to the ranks of the Unworthy."

"So?"

"I can't save you by myself, Jacob. If you don't want to be rescued from the depths of oblivion, there's nothing I can do for you."

"What about that commander guy?" Jake said. "If you don't haul me into that fold, is he going to be ticked because you failed?"

"I'll take my chances. We're making progress here, you and I, and I'd hate for that to go for nothing."

"This is not the kind of work my mother planned for me."

"You've proven your potential by the way you handled the Mary Ann and Georgia matters."

"Yeah, well—" Jake headed for the men's room exit. "Maybe you owe me something too," he said at the door.

The Archangel's sharp response told him how much he thought of that. "What could I possibly owe you?" Jake thought he heard the shocked blinking of Gabriel's eyelashes.

"Bring back those times when Nancy needed me and I wasn't there," he said, "then maybe I could adapt more readily to whatever it is you expect of me. Could you do that for me, Gabe?"

"Don't call me Gabe."

"You got a problem with that? Did your mama call you Gabie Boy when you were growing up?"

"What my—mama—called me, is none of your concern."

"How about it? Do I get those times back so I can do better this time?"

"You know I can't do that."

"How about that boss of yours, that commander guy? Maybe he could do it if you put a bug in his ear."

"He doesn't work that way. He gives you the freedom to work out your own life. It's up to you to decide what kind of man you'll be."

Suddenly across Jake's mind flashed the abusive words of his father.

"Whatcha gonna do when you can't sponge off me no more, boy?" Spike Hannity sneered when Jake was twelve years old. "Huh? Ain't you never gonna grow up and amount to nothin', boy?" He waved a drunken fist that struck Jake on the back of the head. "You gonna be a kid all your life?"

Jake ran from the house, his ears ringing with the sound of his father's jeering voice shouting at his back, "Come back here, junior!" But Jake kept running.

Out the back door he burst, and into the alleyway leading to the Santa Fe tracks. He didn't stop until he heard the mournful sound of the train whistle rousing the world at six o'clock in the morning.

From the time he was a small boy Jake was fascinated by the sound of the wheels click-clacking against the steel tracks, wondering where they came from and where they were going. With a heavy heart, he longed for his dead mother's comforting arms, and wished he could get aboard that train—no matter where it was going.

Jake traded waves with the stripe-capped engineer and waited for the freight to rumble past. He crossed the tracks into Old Town where the shotgun houses of the Negro mill hands lined the dusty, chuck-holed street.

Thin spirals of gray smoke drifted lazily from chimneys sticking out of tin roofs like periscopes. Baying dogs greeted the dawn with their baleful chorus, and from a housetop, a yellow cat observed the early morning parade of sleepy-eyed stumbles toward the backyard privies.

One of those houses belonged to Mussy Mingold, a middle-aged, widowed black woman. For years after Jake's mother died of pneumonia, Mussy picked up a bundle of dirty laundry from the Hannitys' front porch every Monday morning. She brought it back on Tuesday clean and folded.

One Monday morning Mussy didn't come for the laundry. She never told Jake why. She didn't want him to know the last time she went to the Hannity home, Jake's drunken father forced her onto the front room sofa and raped her.

Never again did Mussy come for the laundry, though she and Jake remained friends.

At Mussy's front door he called to her the morning he ran away, seeking solace from his father's abuse. Into her arms she folded the sobbing youngster, pressing his head against her ample bosom.

"You're a good boy, Jacob Hannity," she consoled him, "and don't you never let anybody tell you different." She stroked his brown hair with a palm worn white from a lifetime of labor. "And one day you gonna grow up to be a good man."

That winter Mussy Mingold slipped and fell into a snow drift. By the time they found her, she had frozen to death.

Jake peered for a long moment in the direction from which the voice of the angel came. He wondered if Gabriel knew about Mussy. He did.

"It's not too late," said Gabriel.

"For what?"

"To make her proud."

CHAPTER 8

The Verdict

"There's a call for you, Mr. Whitt." It was Marcus's secretary, Janice Polk, on the intercom.

Marcus was in no hurry to take the call. A glance at his Rolex told him it was two-forty Wednesday afternoon. The hearing was set for two. He knew who was on the line. His attorney, Hank Lassiter, said he would call "when it's over."

Marcus wasn't ready to hear what Lassiter had to say. After fourteen years of marriage, and three strapping sons, his wife Susan told Marcus she didn't want to be married any more. She wanted to pursue her career she said, "Before I get too old."

Marcus wasn't sure which career Susan was so anxious to pursue. Before they married, Susan was a cocktail waitress at his country club. Since the wedding, she kept busy devoting her time and talents to charitable groups, serving tea to the ladies' church circles, volunteering to help at the home for battered women, making herself available to whoever needed a helping hand.

He adored her. He encouraged her to follow her whims wherever they led, and accompanied her to functions she asked him to attend with her.

In the court proceedings, their family attorney, Clay Billings, portrayed Marcus as an absentee father who was rarely home for his sons, an abusive, tyrannical husband whose only interest was his insatiable drive to be the best in the world of business.

Marcus conceded he traveled a lot, but it was necessary in order to build his public relations firm to the standard of excellence he set for himself, to provide a secure future for his family. The allegation of "an abusive, tyrannical husband" was absolutely false, and Billings knew it. Nothing, and no one, meant more to Marcus Whitt than his wife and sons.

The charges were especially shocking since Marcus and Clay were friends since high school. They were members of the same country club, attended church together, and belonged to the same investment group which met at the club twice a month.

Susan and Clay's wife Beth were close friends. They played bridge together, and swam at the club twice a week.

Marcus wracked his brain for some reason Clay would encourage Susan to go through with the divorce. He found none.

Marcus and Susan talked about it, but it was more like a proclamation of her intent than a conversation. She was leaving, moving in with her mother. And, of course, she was taking the boys.

With misgiving, Marcus told himself that sooner or later he would have to pick up the phone, and listen to what he knew would be bad news. Like you know the weed in the woods is poison ivy, but you go there anyway because it's blocking your path. "Hello, Hank."

"It's over, Marcus. She gets half of everything you own. And—" Lassiter took a deep breath, mustering the courage to say, "And sole custody of the boys." The line went silent for a long moment. "Marcus?"

"Am I supposed to thank you for that, Hank?"

"You know I did all I could for you."

"Yes, I knew you would."

"It'll be final in about a month."

Marcus dropped the phone into its cradle. He stroked his chin, and brought his gaze to rest upon the photo of his smiling wife and sons who smiled back at him from the top of his mahogany desk.

CHAPTER 9

Back from the Dead

At seven o'clock in the morning, Georgia Millwood was jarred awake by the ring of the telephone on her bedside table. Awake until all hours the night before, trying to conjure up some way to save James, she finally drifted off to sleep at two o'clock.

With heavy eyelids, she rolled over, wrestled the phone off its cradle, and said hello.

"This is Doctor Finney."

Frantic that something terrible happened to James, her heart leaped. "Yes, doctor?"

"I thought you'd like to know we've found a donor for your husband."

"You what?" She was beside herself with relief. "A donor?"

"Just overnight. A young man was killed in an explosion. He was an organ donor. I knew you'd want to be here."

"What about the money?"

"That's been taken care of."

"Taken care of? How—" She really didn't care how, so grateful was she that a donor had been located for James. Saddened by the reality that someone died and made it possible for her husband to live, in a quiet voice she said, "I'll be right there."

"Good. We'll go ahead with preparations for surgery."

Georgia flipped the phone into its cradle and headed for the shower. At the bathroom door she stopped dead still. She didn't know why. It was like an invisible force had put out a hand and said,

"No need to hurry, there's time."

She glanced over her shoulder, half expecting to see someone behind her. She was struck by a strange thought: The scroungy guy in the noisy camper.

"How much would it take?" he said.

She smiled and shook her head in disbelief. She called him weird.

CHAPTER 10

The Maxed out Card

Deborah Laner pushed her shopping cart into the checkout line at the supermarket.

She hoped there was enough left on her credit card to cover the cost of all the items in the cart: Pens and pencils, a ruler, writing tablet, crayons, construction paper, erasers, a pencil sharpener. Everything she thought her son Eric would need for the first day of school. There was a pile of jeans and tops, socks and a pair of sneakers.

On top of the sneakers was a St. Louis Cardinals baseball cap eight-year-old Eric wanted for the opening of school. In the cart also were a gallon of milk and two loaves of sandwich bread, a five-pound bag of potatoes, a package of ground chuck for hamburgers, and two boxes of Post Toasties.

She came down from the Nikes that Eric begged for to a much less expensive pair of sneakers, and she wasn't even sure she could afford them.

Patiently she waited while the skinny man with a shaggy beard and a gray ponytail in front of her checked through a cart piled even higher than hers. Chatting away with the checker with no regard for the people in line behind him, the gray ponytail wrote a check for his purchases, and departed with an insipid "have a nice day."

When he was gone, Deborah unloaded her purchases onto the conveyor.

The red-haired lady cashier, scanning the items, said, "It looks like you've got somebody starting school too."

"My son Eric," Deborah said. She watched the redhead drag the items across the scanner, running a silent tab, hoping she wouldn't have to put any of them back.

"That'll be $67.82 all together," said the checker.

Deborah slid her credit card through the scanner.

"Is that credit or debit?" the checker said.

"Credit."

"Oops, it didn't work. Let me try it." The cashier took the card, wiped it a time or two against her thigh, and ran it through again. "Oh, Mrs. Laner. It looks like your card is maxed out."

"Maxed out? Are you sure?"

"I'm sorry. Maybe we could put back some of the items you don't need right now."

"I need them all. There's no food in the house, and my son needs these things for school. Are you sure—"

"I wish I could help you," said the checker.

She motioned to a tall, dark-haired woman who stepped over and asked if she could help. Her name was Lela Paget, the supervisor. She listened while the checker explained the problem. Lela spoke briefly with the distraught Mrs. Laner.

To the checker, Lela said then, "Put Mrs. Laner's purchases on my tab." Lela gave the shocked but tearfully grateful Deborah a comforting hug and walked away.

That night Lela explained to her young son, "I'm sorry, Luke. That new bike will have to wait a while longer."

"Aw, mom!"

"I know, honey, but I can't make it this month."

During the night, Lela was wakened by a noise in the front part of the house. Someone at the door? She threw off the covers and grabbed up a robe, wrapped it around her shoulders, and went to investigate. She flipped on the porch light, and eased open the door.

She saw no one. "What in the world—" Leaning against the porch swing was a shiny new bike with Luke's name on it. Attached to the handlebars was a white envelope full of hundred-dollar bills.

"Luke, come here quick!" she called.

A minute later, Luke was out there trying the bike for size. And Lela was thanking somebody she hadn't seen and didn't know for the happy smile on the face of her son. Mystified by her good fortune, she would later try to figure out where the bicycle came from.

"Well done, Jacob," the voice of Gabriel came to him as he settled behind the wheel of the camper parked down the block. "But why did you decide to deliver the bike in the middle of the night?"

"Well, I—I—didn't think she'd want the neighbors to see me in broad daylight."

"See you?"

"You know. If they saw me they'd probably wonder why some tramp was hanging around Mrs. Paget's place."

"Oh?"

"I've been thinking—maybe I should, you know—with all that money, maybe I should buy some new clothes."

"Uh-huh," the Archangel grunted wisely. He wondered how far Jake was prepared to go with that line of thought.

"All this good stuff I'm supposed to be doing," Jake said, "people might appreciate it more if I looked better. Know what I mean, Gabe?"

"Don't call me Gabe."

"Well—"

"We can talk about it later. Right now we have more work to do."

"How's that?"

"There's a man named Marcus Whitt who is in serious trouble and needs to hear from his estranged wife right away."

"Estranged?"

"She filed for divorce, and he doesn't want it. She doesn't want it either, but she got herself in a tangle. Her name is Susan. She's living with her mother—Wilma Castle. You'll find her mother's number in the book."

"You don't know the number?"

"I can't do everything for you, Jacob. Find a phone."

CHAPTER 11

The Call

Susan Whitt never strayed far from the white telephone on the small table in the hallway of her mother's bungalow. For days she anticipated a call from Marcus. She didn't want the divorce, never wanted it, and there were things they needed to talk about. *Why doesn't he call?*

But, she knew Marcus was more apt to go with the flow than to question what he thought she wanted. Whatever Susan wanted, he wanted for her.

Clay Billings pushed her too far too fast. Filing for the divorce was his idea.

"Let me take care of it for you," Clay said.

The next thing Susan knew he drew up the papers—"just a formality"—and brought them for her to sign.

She never intended to go through with the divorce. She went along with it to let Marcus know how much she missed him when he was away for days, sometimes weeks, at a time. She did it to let him know how much his sons needed him at home. She hoped the reality of filing for divorce would jar Marcus into arranging his schedule so he could spend more time with them.

Well aware of Marcus's ambitions, in the beginning she encouraged him to devote as much time and energy as necessary to achieve his goals. Single-handedly he built his PR firm from the ground up. Just last week he landed a major publisher as a client, and remarked to her with great enthusiasm that he was "almost there."

At the Collins's Fourth of July bash, Clay noted she was attending another social event alone, "in widow's black." Clay asked, "Where is the world traveler off to this time?"

With a forlorn expression she explained that Marcus had an appointment with a prospective client in Chicago. She was only half complaining, but there was sufficient distress in her voice to prompt Billings to question whether the sad birds had come to nest in the Whitt household. To his lawyer's ears Susan's complaint smacked of a rift, and the wheels in his head began churning.

Billings long ago was attracted to Susan, and once told her so. She shrugged her shoulders and sluffed it off, attributing his remark to alcohol talk. She never thought of it again.

Billings, with a smirk, lifted another martini from the tray in the hands of Bertha Collins, their hostess. "It appears to me," Billings said to Susan, "you're married to an absentee husband whose time is more valuable than anyone else's."

She pinned him with a sharp look, but his

comment set her to wondering. If other people noticed, maybe her marriage was not as secure as she thought.

Clay kept at her with critical remarks aimed at Marcus, insinuating that he had "other women in other places," and she was being "played for a fool."

Even so, she had second thoughts about the filing. Advised not to contact Marcus until after the divorce became final, she told herself there was no reason he could not call her.

Her reflections were disrupted by the ring of the phone. She snatched it up and said, "Marcus!"

"Mrs. Whitt?" she heard a strange man's voice say, "you need to call your husband."

"My husband?"

"Right now, before it's too late."

"But, I'm not supposed to—"

"Please. You're wasting precious time. Your husband's life is in danger, and he needs to hear from you right now." At the gas station, Jake hung up the pay phone, and breathed a deep sigh. "What's next?" he asked wearily.

"There's always a next, Jacob," said Gabriel. "We never get through."

"How come you don't do some of this stuff yourself, instead of laying it all on me?"

"Because it's your job, not mine."

"How did it get to be my job?"

"Stop complaining, Jacob. What would you be doing if you weren't taking care of the needs of other people?"

"Well, I'll tell you what—"

"You're getting quite good at it," Gabriel said. "How about Mrs. Laner?"

"What about her?"

Into Jake's hand dropped a heavy white envelope.

"Go see if she cares what you look like."

Jake's ears perked up like a setter on point as he approached the front door of Deborah Laner's modest home on the south side of town. Loud voices sifted through the walls, and the last thing Jake wanted was to get involved in a family shouting match. He hesitated before pressing the bell. Before he got a thumb on the bell button, a young boy burst out the door, screaming.

"I wanted Nikes! Everybody has Nikes!"

On the boy's heels his mother ran, crying, "I told you I couldn't afford Nikes this time, honey, but I promise to get them for you as soon as I can." Catching sight of Jake standing apart from the fracas, she covered her mouth with a trembling hand. "Oh!" she gasped.

"It's okay, ma'am," Jake said, raising a calming hand. "I didn't mean to frighten you."

"What are you doing here?" She pushed the boy toward the door. "Eric, get back in the house."

Eric hugged his mother's waist instead.

"Please, don't be alarmed," Jake said. "I'm here to help."

"Help? How could you help me?"

"It's hard to explain, but somebody heard you call."

"I didn't call anybody."

"Last night, ma'am, when you prayed—you

asked for help."

"I always pray after I go to bed," she cried. "It's hard raising my son by myself. I don't understand how you could know that."

From inside his dungarees Jake brought the white envelope. "This is from someone who cares about you—and the boy," he added grudgingly. Jake didn't give half a hoot in a hailstorm about her bratty kid, but his mother needed help. "He wants you to have it," he said, holding the envelope out to her.

"He?" Her face was ashen with fear. "What is that?" She started backing away, pulling the boy with her. "Why would anyone do anything for me?"

"Please, take it. I can't leave until you do."

"No! I don't know what's in that envelope. Who are you?"

"I'm just a messenger," Jake said. "Would you like me to open it and show you what's inside?"

"I—I don't know—I—"

Jake lifted the tab, exposing the money inside the envelope.

"Mom, it's money," Eric whispered, his eyes popping wide.

"Money?" she said. "Where did it come from?"

"Someone gave it to me and told me to deliver it to you. I can't tell you who it was. I'm sorry."

Cautiously she reached out, still not sure she wanted anything to do with the white envelope this strange man in the wrinkled army surplus dungarees was trying to force upon her. In her ears, however, rang the disappointed screams of her son, "I wanted

Nikes!" She reached for the envelope, and with a wary eye briefly checked its contents. With tears streaming down her cheeks, she said to Jake, "I don't know how to thank you?"

"You already have." Jake headed for the camper parked at the curb, climbed inside, drove a block away, and braked to a stop. "I can't do this anymore," he sobbed, resting his head on the steering wheel. "These poor people!"

"Jacob."

"Why are you always hanging around? Don't you ever sleep?"

"It's my job."

"So many problems," Jake moaned. "So much heartache, so much pain."

"That's why you were sent here."

"Well, I don't want to be here."

"If you recall, Jacob, when we first met, you had some unpleasant things to say about your past. You thought you were singled out to bear on your shoulders the weight of the world. Now, you've seen the burdens of other people. Do you still feel losing Nancy was so unbearable you would like to divorce yourself from the human race?"

Jake flipped the angel a questioning look. "What do you mean—divorce myself?"

"Back then you thought you were the only one who had problems, who suffered pain, and so you set out to destroy yourself."

"Is that why you put the finger on me?"

"Partly, but also because the Commander believed you were someone who could relieve the pain and suffering of people less fortunate."

"You picked the wrong man, man."

"That remains to be seen. But you know, Jacob, one who has suffered much understands best the suffering of others. By helping to relieve their pain, yours has become less severe."

"How do you know that?"

The smile in Gabriel's voice did not escape the ears of Jacob Hannity.

"I had a good teacher," said the angel. "Later, Jacob."

"There's always a next," Gabriel had said.

CHAPTER 12

Charlie's Dream

Watching a black teenager shooting hoops on a grassless sand lot, Jake could still hear Eric's screaming protest from the night before, "I wanted Nikes!" and wondered if his part in the Archangel's scheme of things would ever be over.

Charlie Bowles was a slender black sixteen-year-old who didn't like being alone. Yet, every morning before school, and every afternoon when school let out, he was shooting hoops on the vacant lot next to his grandmother's frame house on the edge of town. Alone.

Charlie nurtured the same dreams as most kids his age, including the one of being a star shooting guard in the NBA. Uppermost in his mind, however, was the dream of finding a way to care for his grandmother. She was dying of some disease Charlie couldn't pronounce.

He moved in with his grandmother after his mother died of a drug overdose, and his father went

63

to jail for pushing the drugs that killed her. That's why Charlie was alone, driven to solitude by taunting peers who once were his friends. Thinking, Charlie was. Always thinking. Trying to find a way.

He sank what would have been a three-pointer from beyond the circle, recovered the ball on the first bounce, and went in for a lay-up. Behind him he heard a brief hand clap, and jerked his head around to see who was there. On the sideline, a crumpled up old guy he'd never seen before was squatting with one knee on the ground.

"That's pretty good," Jake said. "Do you do that all the time?"

"Mostly," Charlie said, and sank another long one. "What are you doing here?"

"Watching."

Charlie made a couple more shots. "Go watch someplace else."

"You're pretty good."

"You said that before."

"Who's your favorite player?"

"Shaq."

He kept dribbling, shooting, rebounding. Shooting again.

"He's good all right," Jake said. "I bet some day you could be better."

Charlie gave him a tolerant look. "You're weird, man," he said. "Ain't nobody better'n Shaq."

"How's your grandmother?"

Charlie stopped dribbling and mounted the ball against his thigh. "Why you asking about my grandmama?"

"I heard she wasn't well."

Charlie wondered who this man was. How would he know his grandmama was sick? "Not too good. She needs some medicine, but got no money for it."

"I'm sorry. How about your mother?"

"My mama died."

Jake knew that. He knew all the answers. Gabriel filled him in before he came. He thought the boy might like a chance to talk about it, even to a stranger. But, he didn't ask Charlie about his father, suspecting that might be too painful a subject.

His mother was dead and his father was in jail. Charlie's hope for the future was bleak. Most of what lay ahead for him involved his grandmother who was dying of a disease that the doctors said they couldn't do anything about. And Charlie hadn't yet figured out what he could do about it either.

"I'd like to meet your grandmama," Jake said.

"Why?"

"Maybe I could help her."

Charlie gave his head a dubious shake. He couldn't imagine how this tramp could help anybody. But, the doctors had given up on her, and even the preacher where she went to church stopped coming to see her. This guy in the dingy dungarees didn't look like much, but nobody else offered to help. Maybe he could do something. What did he have to lose?

Without another word, Charlie took his basketball and struck out across the vacant lot toward his grandmama's house.

Jake fell in beside him.

CHAPTER 13

Hello, Hattie

She was lying flat on her back on the front room sofa when Jake stuck out his hand.

"I'm Jake Hannity."

At seventy-seven Hattie Bowles was thin of face and form, but a warm smile lit her wrinkled face when she popped up and took Jake's hand.

"I don't care who you are," she said, sitting upright, "I'm glad to see you. Charlie, get Mr. Hannity something to sit on."

Charlie lifted a cloth-covered footstool and placed it next to the sofa. Jake sat on it, still holding Hattie's bony hand.

"I guess we're old enough that nobody will complain if I hold your hand," Jake said with a grin.

"It don't bother me none," she said, her eyes sparkling. "It looks to me like you could use a friend anyhow. You know, Mr. Hannity—"

"Jake."

"—I don't remember the last time anybody held my hand. Thirteen years ago we lost Charlie's granddaddy in a railroad accident. He worked for the Santa Fe, and never was one to show affection.

"I know he loved me, but he never told me so. The only touching I got from him was in bed when it got so he couldn't stand the pressure anymore.

"He never talked much to anybody. Folks used to say Aaron Bowles was so closed-mouthed, when he died we'd have to find out about it from somebody else." Hattie wiped her eyes, and chuckled, bringing on a spell of coughing.

Jake waited while she composed herself. "Mrs. Bowles," he said. Before he could go on, she smiled and squeezed his hand.

"Lord in heaven," she said, "how good it sounds to be called Mrs. Bowles. I go to the doctor and those twenty-year-old kids call me Hattie. They scream at me like I can't hear it thunder, and say, 'How long have you been sick? Do you remember?' Like I don't have a mind anymore." Again she chuckled and said, "They're good kids though. The young folks are good. They just haven't been taught to respect us old folks." She removed her hand from Jake's. "My, how I do run on, don't I?" she said. "I bet you never came over here to listen to me complain did you, darlin'?"

"Actually, I came because I heard you weren't feeling well."

"Where did you hear that?"

Jake smiled. "A little bird told me."

Hattie laughed and slapped her thigh. "I know about that bird."

"Charlie tells me you need some kind of medication."

"That Charlie! I don't know what in the world I'd do without him. I'd like to send him to college, but there are times when I can't even send him to the store." To Charlie, she said, "Come over here, baby, and hug your grandmama's neck."

Charlie did as he was told, and she wrapped her arms around him. "Yeah," Hattie said after Charlie moved away. "They keep telling me I need this, and I need that. They say I need to go to Mayo's, but I've got no money for Mayo's or anything else. So many doctors don't want to take you anymore if you're on Medicare.

"I was a nurse for forty-three years, and whatever it is I've got now I got from working with the sick folks in the hospital.

"I'm not complaining, Jake. The Lord's been good to me. But when you get old, and they decide they can't do any more for you, they just toss you aside like an old shoe and go to working on somebody else.

"It's not like it used to be. Nowadays most doctors specialize in something or other. They give you sugar pills, or soda pills, or some other kind of pills so you'll think they're doing something for you, hoping you'll go 'way and leave them alone.

"Still, I thank God every day for letting me I live in a country that does its best to take care of us old folks. I don't know what I'd do without that Social Security check on the third of every month. Charlie and I would just dry up and blow away, most likely."

She paused, took a deep breath, and reached for Jake's hand. "You know, Jake," she said, "I don't know how you got here, nor why, but if there were more people like you in this world, it would be a much better place to live."

Jake could think of nothing to say, except goodbye. He patted her hand, and left her with a smile. At the door, he said, "I brought a little something that might help."

On the lamp table beside the door he dropped a white envelope bulging with greenbacks to pay for Hattie's medication, and maybe help some with Charlie's college.

Jake climbed into the camper, his mind on things other than the Archangel, but that's whose voice he heard.

Gabriel cleared his throat to establish his presence. "What do you think now, Jacob?" he said.

Jake jerked his head around, not surprised that the angel showed up. "About what?"

"You made quite a hit with that lady," Gabriel said.

"She's old, she's sick, and probably dying."

"I know. But what you did—and who you are—was what she needed to bring a little joy into her life. In four days, it will be over."

Jake dragged a sleeve across his eyes.

CHAPTER 14

Susan Saves Marcus

Marcus Whitt hardly heard the phone's soft purr. It kept ringing until he stirred awake enough to lift the receiver and hold it to his ear.

"Marcus!"

"Susan?" he said drowsily.

"Marcus, are you all right?"

"No."

"Is something wrong? What are you doing?"

"Dying."

"Dying! Where are you?"

"In our bed. Where are you?"

"Have you taken something? Why did you say you're dying?"

"It's too late, Susan. I'm sorry. It's too late."

"Marcus, I never wanted the divorce."

"I didn't either."

"Clay pushed me into it."

"Okay."

"I'm coming home," she said. "You get up out

of that bed and start walking around."

"Susan—"

"Do it, Marcus! Get out of that bed and on your feet. I'm on my way."

Marcus struggled to throw his legs over the side of the bed. Impelled by the good news that Susan hadn't wanted the divorce, he had to get rid of whatever it was he thought would obliterate the pain of losing her and the boys.

On rubbery legs he stumbled to the bathroom. He knelt beside the stool and plunged a finger into his throat, gagged, and felt the eruption that emptied his stomach. He flushed the stool and watched the deadly white stuff swirl away down the drain.

He was shocked at how close he came to depriving his sons of their father.

CHAPTER 15

Soup and Donald Franklin

Jake stood in the doorway of the City Mission. He surveyed the faces of a dozen people hovering over bowls of hot vegetable soup. Mostly men, some old, some not so old. All with unkempt hair and haggard faces.

Because he was unshaven and sloppily dressed, Jake had no trouble blending in with the others. He thought of Hattie Bowles, and marveled that, diseased as she was, she had lived longer than most of these silent men whose eyes betrayed hopelessness and little promise, who lived one day at a time, whose reward would be seeing the sun come up tomorrow.

He heard no conversation. Their need was for nourishment, not talk. Down on their luck, out of work, broken families, what was there to talk about? The only sound Jake heard was of spoons clicking against metal soup bowls.

At the counter he spotted an elderly man

crumbling crackers between his palms and stirring them into his bowl. Jake knew who he was. Gabriel told him the man's name, what he looked like, and where to find him.

Donald Franklin. Franklin was wearing a blue-and-red checkered shirt buttoned at the collar. His old navy blue coat could have been the top half of a fashionable Austin Reed suit, and his pants were brown corduroy. Franklin was sixty-two years old, but looked ten years older.

Jake eased over that way and parked on a wooden stool beside him. "Morning."

Franklin nodded. "You had soup?" he asked.

"Not yet." Jake grinned. "Is it any good?"

"Not bad." Franklin shrugged. "You take what they give you."

An elderly lady volunteer in a calico apron behind the serving counter flashed a sunny smile. She asked Jake if he'd like a bowl of soup. His camper was stashed with food enough to last a while, and the roadside camp grills came in handy, but the lady was nice enough to offer him soup, so he'd be nice enough to accept it.

"Yes, ma'am, please," he said.

"Bowl or a cup?"

His neighbors were spooning in the food like they hadn't eaten for days, and may not eat again for a while. "A cup will do fine," he said.

"There's plenty," the woman said. "You may as well have more if you want. You look like you could use it."

"Just a cup will do fine, thanks."

She went away, and came back with a cup of

steaming vegetable soup and half a dozen saltine crackers on a paper plate. Jake followed Franklin's lead and crumbled the crackers into his cup. "Do you come here often?" Jake said.

Franklin grinned. "You hitting on me?"

"Oh, no. Just making conversation."

"Here, there, everywhere," Franklin said.

"You don't live around here then?"

"Wherever I am, that's where I live."

Franklin gave his head a thoughtful nod as if trying to remember something. Or maybe trying he was to forget. Jake couldn't tell which.

"I used to live in Illinois," Franklin said. "Decatur. We had a good business going there.

"Plumbing fixtures. Two of us. Then, this other fellow went away to college and learned all there was to know about running the business. When he came back, he discovered for twenty-seven years I did everything wrong.

"We squabbled about that for a while, then he and some lawyers got their heads together and decided I was a drag on the business. This other fellow offered to buy me out, but I didn't want his money. I figured by walking away from it, I was a better man than he was."

When Franklin stopped talking, Jake spooned in a couple of mouthfuls of soup. "You know," he said, "don't you think it's amazing how this world gets stranger all the time?"

"How's that?"

"Well, I heard a story like that about a man and his son who went into business together. They didn't see eye-to-eye on some things, and they parted company. After the older man left, the business started going downhill.

"The son kept it open for a while, but he finally found out his father knew a lot more about the business than he did. By that time the old guy dropped out of sight.

"The boy tried to find him, but didn't know where to look."

The older man shook his head. "Things happen," he said.

"Sometimes kids get to thinking they're smarter than their parents," Jake said. "Like this man and his son I heard about."

"I don't have a son."

"Uh-huh. This man I heard the story about was named Franklin. You might have heard of him. Donald Franklin."

Jake waited for some reaction, but all he got was a brief hesitation of a spoonful of soup on its way to Franklin's mouth.

"His son's name was Gary," Jake said. "Gary Franklin."

Franklin put down his spoon and wiped his mouth with a paper napkin from the chrome dispenser on the counter. With misty eyes he turned to the unkempt stranger on the stool next to him. "Who are you, mister?"

"Jake Hannity."

"Jake Hannity," Franklin said. With a bewildered shake of his head, he said, "I don't believe I know anybody by that name. Have we met before?"

"No, sir. But I know a man named Gary

Franklin who is mighty anxious to catch up with his dad."

"Gary—?"

"Franklin. I thought you might recognize the name."

"Well, it does seem to me that—"

Jake looked away toward the entrance, and nodded to a young man waiting there. Gary Franklin was thirty-three years old, dressed in a gray pin-stripe suit, an apprehensive smile playing at the corners of his mouth. Jake nodded and Gary strode toward where Donald Franklin was crumbling more crackers into his soup bowl.

Gary stopped at the table. "Dad?"

Donald Franklin jerked his head around. He took a long look at the young man staring down at him. With tears streaming down his cheeks, Donald scrambled to his feet, and grabbed his son in a strong embrace.

"I love you, dad," Gary Franklin said.

"I love you too, son."

"I thought I knew everything, but I found out how wrong I was," Gary said. "I want you to come home with me?"

"Home?" his father said. It was a long time ago when he last heard that word.

"Home."

Jake made himself scarce.

In the beginning Jake didn't cherish the idea of playing mediator between a son and the father he hadn't seen for years. He pondered the possibility that the father didn't want to be found. What if the son wanted his father back only because without him the business was going kaput?   Now, along with the warm reunion between father and son, Jake discovered how wrong he was, and his departing steps had a little feel-good spring to them.

"Gabriel?" he said, but got no answer. "That danged angel. He's never around when you need him."

CHAPTER 16

The Missing Link

Vera Spradling's nine-year-old niece Shannon was gone.

Yesterday was Vera's thirty-fifth birthday. Blond, willowy and full of life, she and her husband Steve celebrated with friends for most of the night before. They made the rounds of favorite watering holes. Partying with friends, they didn't get home until the wee hours before dawn.

Wakened by the glare of sun shining through the bedroom window, Vera glanced at the clock on the bedside table. It was straight up twelve o'clock noon. She couldn't believe she slept that late.

Steve had been at the office for hours. Not wanting to wake her, he hadn't told her goodbye when he left. Nor had he called at mid-morning as usual, letting her sleep.

She knuckled the sleep from her eyes, and suddenly remembered her one o'clock appointment with the obstetrician. She was pretty sure of the date, but was anxious for the doctor's opinion as to when her first baby would arrive, sometime in February.

She bounced out of bed, peeled off her nightgown, and headed for the shower.

"That kid!" she said, gathering up the wet towel and soiled clothes strewn over the bathroom floor like a whirlwind had blown through it. She stuck her head out the bathroom door, and yelled upstairs, "Shannon!" She got no answer. Again Vera called, "Shannon, come down here!" Still no answer.

She slung on a robe and marched upstairs, and burst through the door of Shannon's bedroom. "Shannon, when I call, you'd better come running, young lady!" The room was silent. Shannon was not there. "Shannon!"

Vera trooped into every room in the house, upstairs, downstairs, the basement and garage. She held her breath while she checked the pool in the backyard, half expecting to find Shannon's body floating on the water. She breathed a sigh of relief when she saw that it was not. But that only meant Shannon was still gone, and her Aunt Vera didn't know where.

How many times had she warned that kid not to leave the house without telling her where she was going, with whom, and when she would be back? Now there was no note, not anything. Shannon was just gone.

"How was I dumb enough to take her?" she fumed as she made the rounds. "She's Lois's kid, AND Lois's responsibility," Vera muttered, fuming at her younger sister who had taken off three weeks before and left Shannon for her to look after.

Vera grabbed the phone and dialed. When her neighbor answered, she said, "Ashley, is Shannon over there?"

"Shannon? No, she hasn't been here, Vera. Is something wrong?"

"She's not at home, Ashley, and I don't know where she is."

"Was she there this morning?"

"I don't know. We were out late last night, you know, and when I woke up half an hour ago she was gone. The last time I saw her was when Steve and I left to meet you and George last night."

"Oh!" Ashley said. "You left Shannon alone?"

"It's no big deal. We've left her before. She likes being alone sometimes."

"Would you like me to call around? I'd be glad to."

"No, thanks anyway. I'll keep trying to locate her. She's probably at some friend's house. Thanks, Ashley."

"Let me know if I can help."

"I will."

Vera called her other neighbors, Shannon's friends, the church office, the country club. No need to call school. Classes wouldn't start for another two weeks. Nobody had seen nor heard from Shannon since the neighborhood pool party the day before.

Vera was worried, trying not to panic. She called Steve at the office. He tried assuring her that her errant sister's daughter couldn't be far away. "Do you want me to come home?" Steve said.

"No, I guess not. I'll wait a while longer. Maybe she'll show up."

"Then you'd better give her a good talking to."

"Oh, don't worry, she'll get that all right. Dumb kid! Why would she just take off without telling anybody?"

"Why would she take off at all?"

Her doctor's appointment faded in the anxiety over her missing niece.

CHAPTER 17

This is 9-1-1

"You've reached nine-one-one emergency," said a woman's sing-song voice. "Do you have an emergency?"

Steve insisted that Vera call the emergency number, but her hand was shaking so she could hardly dial the phone.

"Yes, I want to report a missing child," she said, feeling the strangeness of doing something she had thought she would never have to do.

"What is your name?"

"Spradling. Vera Spradling."

"And you want to report a missing child?"

"Yes."

"What is your address?"

Oh—uh—1387 Primrose."

"Is that where the child is missing from?"

"Yes, 13—"

"Is that where you are calling from?"

"Yes."

"Is the child a boy or a girl?"

"A girl. She's my niece."

"Her name?"

"Shannon. Shannon Hardwick."

"How old is Shannon?"

"Nine."

"And when was she discovered missing?"

"About noon today."

"It's now 2:48."

"I've been trying to find her."

"And are you now at 1387 Primrose?"

Vera thought the stream of questions would never end.

CHAPTER 18

Chili Dogs & Root Beer

Jake plopped the nozzle into its cradle and replaced the gas cap on the camper. He checked to be sure the passenger side door was ajar in case Bogey decided to hop back in before he returned from paying his bill inside.

The buxom lady behind the counter at the Texaco flashed a big smile and told him he owed. $29.24. Jake tossed a couple of bills on the counter, waited for his change. He slid behind the wheel of his truck, and Bogey greeted him with a toothy grin, panting hard.

Holding the dog on her lap was a young girl with wavy brown hair and green eyes. She was wearing faded jeans, a white cotton top, and white sneakers. Startled at sight of the girl petting his dog on the seat of his camper, Jake said, "Hi."

"Hi," she answered.

"Whose little girl are you?"

"Nobody's."

"Hmmnn. I can't believe nobody would claim a pretty little girl like you."

"Don't condescend to me."

Jake's glance around outside the camper turned up no one who might be looking for a little girl who was sitting in his truck holding his dog.

"Where's your daddy?" he asked.

"I don't have a daddy."

"Uh-huh. How about your mommy?"

"No mommy either."

"No daddy and no mommy?"

"I never had a daddy, and my mommy ran away and left me with some people I don't want to be with. It's no big deal."

"Who are the people you don't want to be with?"

"I'm not telling."

"You won't tell me who they are?"

"No, because you'd make me go back there, and I don't want to go back ever."

Again Jake's eyes sought someone who might rescue him from a ticklish situation. He saw nobody. "I've got to be going now," he said. "Is there some place I can drop you?"

She shook her head no. "There's no place you can drop me."

"Well, you can't stay here, and Bogey and I need to be going."

"I want to go with you."

"That's nice of you, but someone will be looking for you, and I don't want them to find you with me."

"He says I can stay."

"Who?"

"Bogey. He licked my hand."

"Bogey licks everybody's hand."

"That means he likes me."

"I know what it means. I like you too, but—"

"Then that settles it. If Bogey likes me and you like me, it's okay if I go with you."

"It's not that simple. I don't know how to take care of little eight-year-old girls."

"I'm nine and a half, thank you very much. And I can take care of myself."

What was he to do? He couldn't take her with him, and he couldn't forcibly remove her from his truck. "I'll tell you what," he said. "Why don't we stop at that McDonald's over there and have a Big Mac and a Pepsi and talk this over? Are you hungry?"

"Yes, but I don't like Big Macs."

"What do you like?"

"Chili dogs."

"I don't think they serve chili dogs at McDonald's."

"They don't. I've already scoped that out."

"How about the Mexican place across the street? I bet they serve chili dogs."

"Okay."

"We'll go to the Mexican place and have a chili dog and a Pepsi.'

"I don't like Pepsi either."

"What's your favorite drink?"

"Root beer."

"That's it then. I'll buy you a chili dog and a

root beer, and we'll decide what to do next. Okay?"

"I have money."

"Would you like to buy your own?"

"I don't think so. They'd look at us funny."

"Who would?"

"The people in the Mexican place. They'd probably be thinking, hmmmn, why is that sweet little girl buying her own chili dog and root beer when she's with her grandpa?"

"Grandpa!" Jake motioned for her to close the door on her side, and she did. He started the motor, moved the camper onto the street, and found a parking spot in front of the Mexican place.

Inside, they slid into a leather-bound booth, and a young man wearing a white apron and a huge straw sombrero asked what they would like. Jake told him, and he went away.

Over chili dogs and root beer Jake learned the girl's name was Shannon. "I'm Jake Hannity," he said. "Do you have a last name?"

"Yes, but you don't need to know what it is."

Jake decided not to pursue it. Still, if he didn't know Shannon's last name, how could he find out where she belonged? She told him she had run away the night before after the people she was living with left her alone. She also said she spent last night in a packing crate behind the Texaco.

Jake's heart went out to her, since she seemed dead set on escaping an unhappy situation, but the problem of what to do about her didn't go away.

"Jacob." The voice of Gabriel, the Assistant Almighty.

Jake hadn't heard from him for a while. He

wondered if the head angel was called to Headquarters for further instructions, but he had no trouble recognizing the ubiquitous voice.

"What?" Jake said instinctively, noting Shannon's sharp look.

"You must be extremely cautious," the Archangel said. "Your being in the company of this young lady could lead to extenuating circumstances."

"Uh-huh," Jake grunted to avoid further deprecating looks from Shannon.

"I realize this is a difficult time," the angel said, "since she's sitting there looking at you, but I'm not sure I can help you with this one. Already, radio and television stations are broadcasting her name and description. If her whereabouts are not determined soon, the authorities could become seriously involved."

The authorities? Jake almost choked on his chili dog. The last thing he wanted was to get crossways with the law. Not all police officials were as understanding as Officer Goodman.

"You're on your own now, Jacob," Gabriel said. "You would be wise to separate yourself from this young lady as quickly as possible."

The waiter was back, mouthing in broken English the mechanical, "Is everything all right?"

Getting a closer look at Shannon, his eyes bugged out in a flash of recognition from what he heard on the radio. He turned away in a hurry.

Vera's phone hadn't stopped ringing.
She took calls from people she didn't know

who asked questions she already answered.

A police officer dropped by, as did a personable young woman from Social Services, each with more questions. How long had Shannon been missing? When did you last see her? Were other people present? Are there friends or relatives we can contact? Do you think someone might have taken her? If so, who could it have been?

"Please, be patient, Mrs. Spradling," the woman from Social Services cautioned on her way out. "Don't ever lose hope that Shannon will be coming home." She had left Vera a list of phone numbers for radio and TV stations, newspapers, even the FBI, and professional agencies that concentrated on finding lost children.

Vera's body shook like a charred oak leaf in a strong wind for fear night might fall before Shannon was found. The worst always happened after dark. She tried convincing herself that her niece had not been kidnapped. The fact that Shannon didn't belong to her no longer mattered. Nor did it matter that her wayward sister had dumped her daughter in her lap and run off with that lab technician from Arizona.

What did matter was that Lois thrust upon her the responsibility of caring for her offspring, and Vera had come up short. The police officer told her if Shannon was abducted, whoever took her could have disappeared at a mile a minute, and there is no time to lose.

Her fingers were numb from dialing. Three more times she called Steve for advice and encouragement, but he was out of the office. She paced the floor, checking the front window every few minutes, expecting to see Shannon strolling nonchalantly up the walk at any moment.

Staring at the phone, she willed it to ring, bearing Shannon's voice.

"Shannon, where are you?" she screamed at the big picture window overlooking the backyard, trying to hang on.

"If you lose hope, so will everybody else," she was admonished by some faceless voice on the phone, someone who likely had not experienced the helplessness of locating a lost child who didn't belong to her.

"You are in charge," the voice assured her.

"I don't want to be in charge!" Vera wailed, hanging up the phone. "I want somebody to find my niece!"

Another trip to the big window, and she was shocked at what she saw. Her backyard was full of people! What were they doing there? Nobody contacted her.

Ashley Whitworth, her closest friend and neighbor, was gesturing with both hands as if signing to a class of deaf people. Ashley pointed and waved her arms. She appeared to be issuing instructions to the people scurrying around, eager to do whatever she told them.

Vera dashed through the kitchen to the garage's back door, but by the time she got there, Ashley and her charges had fanned out like Marines closing in on a pillbox.

She wanted to find out from Ashley what she was up to, but it was too late. Into the woods back of the house they marched with Ashley leading the way, like Stanley searching for Livingston in the African bush, combing every foot, every plant and tree for signs that Shannon might be, or had been, there.

The search went on. The people swarmed over parks and playgrounds. No private property was off limits. Neighbors and residents up and down the street, even on streets blocks away, opened their doors to basements, attics, and garages, seeking the whereabouts of the missing Shannon. Wherever a child might hide or be hidden, the crusaders stormed through.

While Vera yearned for positive news of Shannon's whereabouts, dozens of people, including law enforcement, family agencies, and broadcasters, were planning strategy, covering whatever contingency might be encountered in their search for the errant child. Radio and telephone lines were kept open to the highway patrol, Amber Alert, and other missing children's networks. Posters were distributed to movie theaters, playgrounds and restaurants, and public places where an abductor might be sighted with a small child. Newspaper accounts of Shannon's disappearance were rushed to publication.

As soon as she hung up from 9-1-1, Vera dialed Tony Harlow, news director of Rock 93 FM, Shannon's favorite radio station.

Harlow was eager to help. "What we do here is not official," he told Vera, "so I'll have to check with the police to verify whatever they have on Shannon's disappearance."

"But, don't the police have a waiting period before they do anything in cases like this?" she said woefully.

"That's true in some departments, Mrs. Spradling, but I still need to check with them. We don't want to interfere with any action they might be planning."

"What can I do?"

"Stay by the phone, and pray that she's some place where they can find her. After I talk to the information officer over there—that's Sergeant Brady—I'll give you a call."

"Will that take long?"

"That depends on how soon I can reach Brady. But I can tell you this much: Once we get the go-ahead, we'll interrupt programming every fifteen minutes with a description of Shannon, listing your phone number, as well as the police emergency line."

"Thank you."

"Don't expect too much too soon. Sometimes these things work pretty fast, and other times it takes longer.

"Shannon is out there some place, and she probably has been seen by several people. Hopefully, one of them will give us a call. All right, Mrs. Spradling?"

"Thank you so much."

Shannon was Lois's kid, Vera fumed, and she should be there helping look for her. Vera called her mother in New Jersey, trying to locate Lois to let her know Shannon was missing. Her mother had neither seen nor heard from Lois since she left three weeks ago.

"Is there anything wrong?" her mother said with concern in her voice.

Vera skirted the subject, not ready to admit that she had been negligent in caring for her sister's offspring. She tried to convince herself that Shannon would show up at any time, in which case she wouldn't have to tell her mother that her granddaughter had disappeared.

Tony Harlow kept his promise. He had broadcast the bulletin every fifteen minutes since mid-afternoon. Vera fielded numerous calls from people who thought they had seen Shannon in different places all over town. Grateful as she was for their concern, her hand was numb from holding the phone. Even so, no call went unanswered, as she held out hope that the next one would be from Shannon. She was shocked when it came.

CHAPTER 19

Return of the Prodigal

Jake snarfed the last bite of his chili dog, then drained his root beer glass. Shannon devoured hers as though she hadn't eaten for days.

"You're a very nice young lady," Jake said, "and I wish there was something I could do for you, but I think we had better be letting someone know where you are."

"No, please," Shannon said with tear-filled eyes. "I want to go with you."

"Shannon, I would like nothing better than to have you ride along with Bogey and me, but I don't think you understand how serious this could be if they found you here. I can't allow you to go with me, and I don't want to dump you on the street. So, you need to tell me where you came from, so I can take you back there."

"No, Jake, please," she cried, "I don't want to go back there."

"It's not safe for you to be running around by

yourself, with no one to look after you. I can't leave you here to do that."

What did he know about dealing with a nine-and-half-year-old runaway kid anyway? Nothing. He never had one, didn't want one, never would have one, and didn't like the situation that was forced upon him—the responsibility of doing something about this kid who begged to go with him. Still, Jake could not shirk the need to get Shannon into safe hands.

Why had that angel just bugged off and left him alone to figure this thing out on his own? "Shannon, I bet if you called home, they'd be so glad to hear from you they would never treat you bad again."

Shannon's lower lip curled up, and she wiped her eyes with the back of her hand. Jake ripped a paper napkin from the dispenser and helped her wipe.

"If you don't call home," he said, "I'll have to call somebody and let them know where you are. If the police find you with me, I could be put in jail, and I don't think you want that, do you?"

"No," she sobbed, "I don't want you to go to jail. What would happen to Bogey?"

"Well, then?"

She sniffled and wiped while she thought about that. "Okay, Jake," she sobbed.

"Okay what?"

"Okay I'll call."

Jake breathed a relieved sigh, and handed her a quarter for the phone in the booth next to the cashier.

"Aunt Vera?" he heard Shannon say into it.

"Shannon! Where are you?"

"With Jake and Bogey."

"Jake? Jake who? Who is Bogey?"

"Jake is my friend. He bought me a chili dog and root beer."

Vera was visibly shaken, so relieved was she to know that Shannon was alive. "Shannon, listen to me," she said. "Your Uncle Steve and I have been worried sick about you. Tell me where you are, and we'll come bring you home."

"You don't have to do that."

"Yes. We want you here."

"Jake will bring me."

"Jake? Who is Jake? Are you sure? Shannon, are you all right?"

"I'm fine," Shannon sniffled, "but I don't want you to yell at me anymore."

"I promise. All you have to do is come home, and I will never yell at you again."

"Okay bye."

"Shannon!"

She hung up the phone and said to Jake, "She says it's okay."

Vera spread her arms and shouted, "She's coming home!"

Steve was at the office when she called. "Shannon just called. She's coming home!"

"I'll be right there!" he said, grabbing his jacket on the way out.

Friends, neighbors, and well-wishers who heard the news on the radio ringed the cul-de-sac, awaiting the arrival of the young girl for whom they had spent much of the day searching. Among them were people Vera didn't know, curiosity seekers eager to be a part of a news-making event. All eyes focused on the entrance to the cul-de-sac where a dirty camper with pots and pans bouncing off its sides crawled toward them.

"Is that it?" Steve said, scowling at the mud-splattered pickup.

"I didn't think it would look like that," Vera said.

"It looks like a trash wagon."

"Never mind. She's coming home."

Sergeant Brady had taken the call from the waiter at the Mexican restaurant, and alerted police cars in the area. "We've got the subject under surveillance," he had said to police cruisers in the area. "Do not attempt to apprehend the individual. Repeat: Do not attempt to apprehend the subject, but keep him in sight. We don't know if he is armed, but we can't take a chance on harming the girl. Proceed with caution."

Four black-and-white cruisers answered the call, and fell in line half a block behind the camper.

Jake turned onto Primrose two blocks from the Spradling home and spotted the cruisers in his rear view mirror.

"Police cars," he said with a puzzled shake of his head.

"What are they doing here, Jake?" Shannon said.

"I don't know," Jake said. "There must be something big going on around here."

He was suddenly struck by the notion that the

police cruisers might be following him. Had they learned that Shannon was with him? How would they know? If they were after him, why didn't they just pull him over? Did they need that many police cars to keep a dirty camper in sight? He was bringing Shannon home, for crying out loud. It wasn't like he was holding her for ransom. What more did they want?

Shannon was silent for most of a minute before she said, "Jake, I need to ask you something."

"Okay."

"Are you a bum?"

He kept an eye on the cruisers in the rear view. They weren't getting any closer, so they must not be after him. "You might say that," he answered. "There are different kinds of bums, Shannon. Some bums are just bums, you know, because they like living that way, and they don't have to answer to anybody. Some are out of work and looking for more, so they're not real bums. Then there are us no-goods who have no place to go and nothing to do when we get there. We like the freedom of going where we want when we want without asking anybody if it's all right." He wondered briefly into which category Gabriel had pigeon-holed him. And, come to think of it, where was that haughty Archangel? Was he observing the proceedings from afar, or had he deserted him altogether?

"Some of us are lucky enough," Jake said, "to run across a nice little nine-year-old girl like you—"

"Nine and a half."

"—who brings some sunshine into our lives and makes it all worthwhile."

"I love you, Jake."

He nodded and smiled. He hadn't heard those words for much too long. He didn't try to hide the mist in his eyes. "We all need somebody to love, don't we?" he said.

The camper cleared the mouth of the cul-de-sac. Two black-and-whites pulled to a stop, blocking the entrance so the camper couldn't escape. The other two cruisers eased over and parked near where the crowd waited.

"There they are," Shannon said to Jake.

"Who?"

"Aunt Vera and Uncle Steve."

"Who are all those other people?"

"I don't know. Oh, there's Aunt Vera's friend Ashley. What's she doing here?"

"Are you okay, Shannon?" He braked to a stop in the middle of the turn-around.

"Okay, Jake." She wiped her eyes, and gave Bogey a hug. "Will I ever see you again?"

"I hope so. Ever is long time. Remember, you're a big girl now. You can take care of yourself."

"You in the camper," said a reverberating voice on a bullhorn. "You're surrounded by law enforcement officers. Do not try to escape. Let the girl go, then step out of the vehicle with your hands up."

"You better go now," Jake said to Shannon.

"I don't want to go."

"I know."

She patted Bogey on the head. He yipped his approval, and gave her a parting lick on the face.

"Bye, Jake."

She pecked him on the cheek, and they traded hugs. Shannon hopped down out of the truck.

Vera and Steve rushed forward to grab her.

"Do not approach the vehicle!" It was Lieutenant Clyde Farmer, holding the bullhorn to his mouth.

The Spradlings stopped in their tracks, and waited for Shannon to come to them. Vera grabbed Shannon in a grateful hug. "What did he do to you?" she said.

"Nothing," Shannon said.

Steve, a big man with a balding pate, demanded, "What did he threaten you with?"

"Nothing!"

"The child has been brainwashed," said a big-nosed woman in a green hat. "It's obvious she has been threatened, and is afraid to talk about it."

"You in the camper," the bullhorn blared again. "Step out of the vehicle slowly, with your hands up."

"Jacob."

Now he shows up!

"Where were you when I needed you?" Jake said.

"Never mind. You just do as you're told."

"Why? I haven't done anything."

"I know that, and you know that, but those men with the guns don't know that. Now, step out of the camper with your hands up."

Slowly Jake pushed open the door and climbed down onto the concrete driveway. With his hands in the air, he was shocked to be looking into the muzzles of half a dozen service revolvers.

"Back away from the vehicle slowly, five paces," the bullhorn commanded.

The crowd watched Jake follow the advice of the Archangel, doing as he was told.

"Now, turn around and face this way," said the bullhorn.

Jake wasn't sure which way "this way" was, but he turned to his right and saw the bullhorn sticking out of the face of a uniformed officer thirty feet away. Three officers closed in on him. Two of them grabbed his arms and held him while the third man yanked Jake's hands behind his back, and clamped handcuffs on his wrists. They started shoving him toward a police car.

"No!" Shannon cried. She tried to break away, but Steve grabbed her arm. "He's my friend!"

Out of the crowd stepped a black woman, waving her arms. It was Georgia Millwood. "Just a minute, officer," she said.

Lieutenant Farmer cast her a curious look, held up a hand and the three officers relaxed their hold on Jake's arms. "What is it, ma'am?" Farmer asked.

"That man is no criminal," she said.

She heard the radio description of the camper, and recognized it as belonging to the man who wanted to help get her off the street.

"That man saved my husband's life," Georgia said.

Farmer studied the woman. "And how did he do that, ma'am?"

"With fifty thousand dollars."

The crowd gasped with hands to mouths.

Farmer said, "I find it hard to believe this man could come up with fifty thousand dollars." He tossed a derisive grin at his colleagues, and they matched it with their own.

"Officer," came another voice. Mary Ann Bracker stepped forward and said, "I too can testify as to the good character of this man."

"How's that, ma'am?" Farmer was puzzled.

"I lost my job, and with three little kids to feed, I had nowhere to turn. This man came knocking on my door and gave me an envelope full of hundred-dollar bills. Ten thousand dollars' worth!"

Farmer wondered if there was a bank holdup he hadn't heard about. What was the matter with these people? He caught a suspect in the act of endangering the life of a little girl, maybe even kidnapping and they were trying to make him believe this bedraggled individual committed no crime.

The lieutenant was on the verge of ignoring the women's pleas when from the crowd stepped a gray-haired man in clean, creased khaki pants and a yellow knit shirt.

It was Donald Franklin. Beside him stood his son Gary, wearing a navy blue jacket and light blue pants. "Hold on there, officer," Donald said. "This man might have saved my life too." He placed an arm across his son's shoulders. "If it hadn't been for Jacob Hannity, I might have spent the rest of my life believing my son never wanted to see me again. Thanks to him, we found each other."

"Jacob."

Jake was concentrating on what was going on,

but he wasn't too busy to hear the voice of the Archangel.

"What is it?" he asked mechanically.

Eight police officers and dozens of onlookers stared at him, having heard nothing.

"Scratch your nose," Gabriel said.

"What!"

"Scratch your nose, Jacob."

Under his breath, Jake muttered, "Scratch my nose? With my hands tied behind me, how do you think I could—"

"Jacob, lift your left hand and scratch—your—nose."

Jake tried moving his left hand, and was shocked when it slipped free of the handcuffs. He used it to scratch his nose. The cops stared, not believing what they saw. Jake couldn't believe it either.

An officer checked the cuffs and found the left one dangling loose. He tried to re-fasten it around Jake's wrist, but it wouldn't lock. He took another pair from his partner, but they wouldn't lock either.

"What's the problem, Wilson?" Farmer barked.

"The handcuffs won't lock, sir."

"Well, try another pair."

"I did, but they don't lock either."

The crowd stirred impatiently as more handcuffs were tried, but none locked. Their attention was drawn to the two black-and-whites blocking the cul-de-sac's entrance. The cruisers began easing away, leaving the entrance wide open.

"Who moved those cars?" Farmer demanded. "I gave no order to move those cars!" Realizing all officers were accounted for, he decided someone had tried to make off with the cars, and ordered two men to pursue.

With drawn weapons they charged the cars, and found neither had a driver.

"What's going on here?" Farmer barked.

Eight service revolvers leaped from their holsters and were aimed at Jake Hannity's chest. Eight guns suddenly went flying from the hands of the astonished officers who tried to haul them in. The stunned crowd tried to figure out what was going on.

Confusion reigned as into Jake's hand dropped the keys to his truck.

"That officer over there took them," Gabriel said. "Now, Jacob, I want you to get in the truck, start the motor, and drive away from here."

"Drive away? They'll fill me full of lead!"

"Not without weapons. Just do as I say."

"What have you done here? I can't just—"

"Yes, you can. Would I lie? Go, Jacob. Now!"

Jake leaped into the truck, and started the motor, expecting at any moment to be riddled by a volley of gunshots. The guns were still flying around like angry bees with a bunch of exasperated cops trying to grab them from mid-air.

Jake wheeled the camper around, headed for the exit, and waved at Shannon as he went. Bogey barked goodbye for good measure.

"Bye, Jake," Shannon called after them. Cupping her hands to her mouth, she said, "Bye, Bogey. I love you!"

CHAPTER 20

So Long Angel

Jake was headed west into the sunset when to his ears came the voice of the Archangel. "You were lucky to get out of that mess alive."

"Thanks to you," Jake said, and kept driving.

"It wasn't my doing. I was only following instructions."

"Oh?"

"It seems you survived the probationary period, and are cleared to advance to the next level."

"Well, that sure is good news," Jake said with a tinge of irony.

"Don't be smart, Jacob. You're not out of the woods yet."

"So, what are you lining up for me now?"

"Not a thing."

"What! Does that mean I've outlived my usefulness?"

"Not at all. The Commander informs me you have earned a bit of R & R."

"Really? And what will happen to all that money left over from wherever you got it if I decide to make this R&R permanent?"

"You dare not. And the money will be in safekeeping until you return."

"From where?"

"Wherever you want to go."

"Well," Jake said with an approving nod. "I've always wanted to see the ocean."

That was not totally true. He would as soon camp out with Bogey beside some stream with a hook in the water. But, because Nancy couldn't see the ocean, he would keep his promise to her and take a look at it for both of them.

"Go for it, Jacob. But remember—the Commander has plans for you, and you've come too far to blow it all away."

Jake smiled, and said, "You know, Gabe—"

"Don't call me Gabe."

"—with a little effort, I could learn to like you."

"Uh-huh," said Gabriel.

Jake thought he heard a hint of humor in the voice of the angel.

"I wish I could say the same for you. Later, Jake!"

"Don't call me Jake."

Jake pointed the nose of the camper down the road into the sunset.

He wasn't sure where he'd find the ocean, nor how long it would take to get there. But, of one thing he was sure—wherever the road led, that angel would be hanging around somewhere.

ABOUT THE AUTHOR

An accomplished author with many books to his credit, David A. Estes draws on his wide experience, from the cotton fields of Oklahoma and Texas where he grew up, to the islands of the South Pacific where he served as a United States Marine, to the market place in America where he retired from a career in broadcasting.

David writes westerns and mysteries, along with many other genres of novels and short stories. He lives on his family farm in West Central Missouri with two black Labs and a suspicious cat.

Other publications
by David A. Estes:

Available at Amazon, B&N, Kobo and other
online retailers.

Blood on the Wall
Bye Bye, Sweet Susie
A Bag of Gold
Wet Dogs Don't Ride (aka Lincoln Beck)
Ajax and Elbow Grease
Angel on My Back

www.davidaestes.com